From the very beginning of her new career as surgery nurse in beautiful Cumbria, Teresa Denning found herself at daggers drawn with the senior partner, Kiel Braden. But Teresa knew her heart was more vulnerable to the feelings she had for Keil than to the disappointment in her job . . .

A COMPELLING FORCE

It hadn't taken Ivory Weston long to fall in love with Jacob Pendragon. But was the compelling force she felt only on her side, or did Jacob feel it as well?

SECOND ENCOUNTER

Jancy's first encounter with love and Saxon Marriot had brought nothing but pain, with his contemptuous rejection. A cruise seemed like the ideal break, a respite from the heartache ... but Saxon was there too, and there could be no escape from this shipbound second encounter ...

IMPULSIVE CHALLENGE

On principle, Gisele disliked and distrusted everything about Nathaniel Oakley: he was just the kind of man who had caused her so much heart-searching in the past. But then she found herself having to pose as his fiancée. Thrown so intimately into his company, would even Gisele be able to resist him?

AT DAGGERS DRAWN

BY

MARGARET MAYO

MILLS & BOON LIMITED
15–16 BROOK'S MEWS
LONDON W1A 1DR

First published in Great Britain 1986
by Mills & Boon Limited

© Margaret Mayo 1986

Australian copyright 1986
Philippine copyright 1986
This edition 1986

ISBN 0 263 75389 1

Set in Monophoto Plantin 10 on 11 pt.
01–0686 – 53211

Printed and bound in Great Britain by
Collins, Glasgow

CHAPTER ONE

THE bang startled Terri and it took all her strength to hold the car on a straight course. Cursing inwardly, she stopped and climbed out. Of all the days to get a puncture!

The road, snaking ahead like grey ribbon, was deserted. Typical, she thought bitterly, just when help was needed. High fells rose on either side, in the far distance, water glinted. But where were the thousands of holidaymakers who were supposed to haunt the Lakes at this time of year? Why was there no one about?

With a sigh Terri unlocked the boot and heaved out the trolley-jack her brother had given her for her last birthday. Not that she had appreciated it at the time, she would much rather have had something to wear. But now she thanked Richard for his thoughtfulness. She also blessed him for giving her a few lessons in basic car maintenance.

She was on her knees struggling with a particularly stubborn nut when a deep male voice penetrated her concentration. 'Can I be of any help?'

Terri jumped violently, having heard no one approach, and observed a pair of shiny black shoes only inches away. Her eyes travelled up a long length of leg clad in grey well-cut trousers, past narrow hips to a pair of capable-looking hands, thumbs hooked into trouser-tops. A white shirt covered a powerful chest, open at the collar to reveal a deep teak tan and a smattering of sun-bleached hair.

Eventually she reached the stranger's face.

Disappointingly, his eyes were hidden behind a pair of dark glasses which sat over a long straight nose. His lips were full and sensual, twisted into an appreciative smile. Tawny hair grew low over his forehead.

Slowly Terri stood up, brushing back her own heavy silver-blonde hair. Her cheeks were flushed and her unusual amethyst eyes large and luminous. 'I don't normally have this trouble,' she said savagely. 'I don't know what's wrong with the wretched nut.'

'You look too frail to be even attempting to change a wheel.' His voice was a velvet-soft growl, coming from somewhere deep in his throat. 'What on earth made you think you could do it?'

Terri put her hands on her hips, indignantly drawing herself up to her full five foot six, tilting her chin to look into the man's face, ignoring the strong masculine dynamism that was making itself felt. 'I'm not a helpless female, I can assure you. There's no point, is there? There's not always a convenient male around.'

'It's lucky for you I'm here now.' There was laughter in his voice, no indication that her sudden hostility offended him.

She wished he would take off his sunglasses so that she could see the expression in his eyes. 'Maybe if you could undo that one nut? I don't like to trouble you, I know I'm capable, but I'm starting a new job and it would be awful if I was late. A puncture sounds such a lame excuse.'

Terri knew she was talking too quickly, but this man had an unusually disturbing influence. She felt sure that behind those dark glasses he was mentally stripping her naked.

'I'm certain no man could fail to believe you,' he said. 'Especially when you turn up with that delightful smear of oil across your face. It will add credibility to your story.'

'Oh, Lord!' Terri felt momentarily horrified. 'That means I shall have to stop somewhere and clean up. I'll be even later!'

'One look out of those beautiful violet eyes and all will be forgiven.' He squatted and turned the wheel-brace with effortless ease. 'You're worrying for nothing.'

'I shall worry if I lose this job.'

He pulled off the wheel and stood up, his smile warm and sincere. 'I'm sure no one would have the heart to do that to you.'

'I hope you're right,' said Terri, 'and thanks. I can manage now.'

'I wouldn't dream of it. Changing wheels is no job for a lady.'

Terri jutted her chin. 'I'd have been in a pretty pickle if I couldn't have done it and you hadn't come along. I'd have been here all day—or had a mighty long walk. I don't understand why you think a woman shouldn't do these things. The only reason you men think we're incapable is because you've made us that way.' She glared at him angrily. Men like him made her mad!

'So you're one of those liberated women?' He looked amused as he swiftly and deftly positioned her spare wheel.

'It depends what you mean by liberated.' Terri watched as he worked. He had nice, well-shaped hands, his nails short and clean. Capable hands. 'I still like a man to open doors for me and hold my coat. I love feminine clothes and expensive perfume, and yet I'm not averse to donning trousers and sweater and getting down to a job if the occasion demands.'

He turned his head and looked up, grinning widely,

his teeth white and even, if a little on the large side. 'You're very positive. I like that.'

She could feel the electric vitality of this stranger and wished yet again she could see his eyes. It was disconcerting, talking to someone and not being able to see them clearly. She liked to know what a person was thinking, liked to judge their reactions by their expressions. There was no way of telling what this man thought. He seemed to find her amusing, that was for sure, and she was not certain she cared very much for that.

But he was doing her a favour. She could have been here for hours wrestling with that nut—and there was no denying he was attractive. Not that it mattered; she was hardly likely to see him again.

'The way I look at it,' she said, 'there's a for and against for everything. If a woman wants to do a man's job and forgo her femininity then that's up to her. I like to achieve a happy medium. I don't think there are many women who are totally feminine and refuse to lift a hand to help themselves. Is that the sort you like?'

She was being impertinent, she knew, but she believed in speaking her mind, whether to a friend or a complete stranger.

He stood up, straightening his back, and again Terri grew aware of his powerful physique, his magnetic personality. There was certainly no ignoring this man.

'It seems you're trying to tell me that the old-fashioned type of woman is no good? I must admit they're thin on the ground these days. Not that the beautiful, helpless type appeals to me. I like a woman with intelligence, a sparring partner, a mental companion. Have you any suggestions?'

Oh, how she wished she could see his eyes. Was he making fun of her, or was there a double meaning behind his words? He was standing a little closer than was surely necessary? She could smell his expensive aftershave and was alarmed to feel shock waves of awareness run through her.

'You're not married, then?'

He shook his head. 'I haven't had the time.' He shot back his cuff and glanced at his watch. 'Even now, like you, I'm running late. Don't forget to get that tyre seen to as soon as possible.' He tidied everything away, his actions quick and confident, wiped his hands on a rag, and shut down the boot lid.

Terri's breathing deepened and her heart played an erratic tattoo. He was a positive, assertive type such as she had never met before. An irresistible type. She held out her hand. 'Thank you for your help, Mr— er——?'

He grinned. 'Let's dispense with formalities. My name's Kiel—and you are?'

'Terri.' She looked at the dark lenses, the tops of which were brushed by his hair, and tried to ignore the electric charges shooting through her. His grip was firm and warm. 'I'm very grateful. I might have still been struggling if you hadn't stopped. I hope I haven't held you up too long?'

He let go of her hand with a smile. 'It's worth being late to make your acquaintance—Terri. Maybe we'll bump into each other again? I get around quite a bit.'

'I think I'd like that,' she said, and realised she meant it. 'I really must make haste now. Thanks again for changing the wheel.' She slid into her car and started the engine, noting through her rear-view mirror that he stood and watched until she was out of sight.

Not until then did she realise she was holding her breath. She let it go and slowly brought the car to a halt.

Her hands were clammy as she delved into her bag for a packet of tissues.

She had never before met a man who had had such an immediate effect—even Greg, who she had thought she loved enough to marry, had not had this instantaneous visual impact.

She rubbed at the oil on her forehead, shocked by the glow in her cheeks, the brightness to her eyes. Could one brief meeting with a total stranger really do this to her? Wasn't she past this sort of thing? It was illogical, stupid, insane. And as there was no likelihood of her seeing him again, even though he seemed to think so, she must push all thoughts of him from her mind. She must concentrate instead on creating the right impression when she arrived at the clinic.

She had never expected to get the job, had been surprised and pleased when Dr Braden wrote offering it without even taking the trouble to interview her. Her references, he said, were excellent.

Richard had said there was no need for her to move, that they could all three share the house, but she felt sure he was only being kind. What newlyweds wanted a third person living with them?

So when she heard about this job as nurse/receptionist in a country doctor's practice in the Lake District she applied for it. It would be bliss to be away from the madding crowd. So much had happened over the last two years that even living in a desert sounded preferable.

She set the car into motion again, and as she approached Lake Windermere, her breath caught in her throat. Viewed through a framework of feathered branches it was dramatically beautiful. Volcanic hunchbacked mountains towered majestically above smaller rounded tree-covered hills, which sloped right down to the shores of the lake itself. Its surface was dotted with boats whose sails were as brilliant as butterflies.

Terri would have liked to linger, but knew she must go on, even though it was the most spectacular scene she had ever witnessed. There would be other occasions for admiring the Lakes.

Finally, after stopping several times to ask her way, Terri arrived. It was nothing like the modern impressive health centre she had left behind. A converted barn, by the look of it, with a brass plate outside one of the doors. Dr K. J. Braden. Dr B. Allen.

Dr Braden, the senior partner, who had written offering her the job. He sounded nice, and she imagined him to be an elderly white-haired gentleman who had tended the sick in this area for a good many years.

And Dr Allen—Barry. Recently qualified and a friend of her brother. It was he who had told Richard about the job, but Terri had not mentioned his name when applying in case it looked as though she was seeking a favour.

A door opened as she pulled up and Barry launched himself at her. Terri had known him for as long as she could remember. He had faded out of their life when he went to medical college, but he had never completely lost touch, even if it was only a card at Christmas.

He gave her a swift bear-like hug. 'I expected you earlier.' His brown hair was as untidy as ever, his arms and legs long and gangling. He must be nearly thirty now, she thought, yet he still had that boyish grin that never failed to get him his own way.

'I had a puncture,' she said at once, 'and I so wanted to make a good impression. Is Dr Braden very annoyed? I hope not—I don't want to start off on the wrong foot.'

'Relax!' He held her at arm's length, his sultry dark eyes observing her with amusement. 'He's out at the moment and has asked me to welcome you and show you around.'

Terri let out a sigh of relief. 'Thank goodness, and congrats on becoming a fully-fledged doctor. I'm very impressed. I never thought you'd make it.' Barry was not the serious kind, always laughing and joking and not seeming to care whether he made anything of his life or not.

'There's faith for you,' he grumbled good-naturedly, leading her inside. 'Now, tell me what made you come up here? I couldn't believe it when I discovered who our new nurse was going to be.'

'*You* told Richard about it,' she said, 'but if you mean why have I left London—peace and quiet's what I want right at this moment. You've no idea how much I'm looking forward to it.'

She followed him into a waiting-room that was surprisingly light and airy with a tank of tropical fish in one corner.

'Not what you expected, eh?' He smiled, observing her raised eyebrows. 'There's been no expense spared, I can tell you. This is my consulting room, and this is my—er—partner's.'

There was a marked difference between the two. Barry's was tiny and cramped, the other extremely spacious. 'Why?' she questioned.

He shrugged. 'Originally there was just one doctor. I've been pushed into the only room available.'

'But is that fair? If there are too many patients for Dr Braden why doesn't he provide adequate facilities for you?'

'Perhaps I have to prove my worth,' said Barry drily. 'Don't forget, I haven't been here long.'

Terri said no more, but still thought it unjust.

'And here is your domain,' he went on, opening a door marked *Nurse*.

It was a relief to see it was well equipped. Terri had had her doubts when she saw the building from outside.

'And the reception area,' continued Barry. 'Medical records, telephone, and so on,' waving his hand expansively. 'Think you can cope?'

'I hope so.' She smiled. 'I've given up a good job. What's Dr Braden like?'

He pulled a wry face. 'Most people like him.'

'But you don't?' She frowned quickly, sensing dissension. Perhaps he was one of the old school, a bit set in his ways and not too keen on the ideas and methods of a newly qualified doctor.

He shook his head quickly. 'He's all right. *You'll* like him.'

Terri hoped so. She was suddenly unsure whether she had done the right thing in accepting this job without first coming to see for herself who she would be working with and what the place was like.

Not that she had any worries about the set-up. It was idyllic, right on the outskirts of Windermere. Not too far for people to travel, and yet with the countryside on the doorstep.

But she was concerned about Dr Braden. Barry had instilled doubts. His letter had been polite and welcoming, now she wondered. What sort of a man was he?

But she pushed her vague unease to one side. 'Show me where I'm to live. The doctor said there was a flat available if I wanted it.'

Barry looked suddenly guilty. 'There's been a slight

hitch. I'm using the flat myself, you see. I was supposed to move out, but I haven't yet found anywhere suitable.'

'Oh, Barry!' Terri looked at him in dismay. 'Now what am I going to do?'

'You could——' He broke off as a car screeched to a halt outside. Seconds later the door opened and to Terri's amazement the tall, fair stranger who had come to her rescue appeared.

'I thought I recognised the car. Don't tell me *you* are Teresa Denning?' He snatched off his glasses as he strode into the room and Terri found herself looking into a pair of steely grey eyes. They pierced her through and through, convincing her she had not been mistaken when she thought he was disrobing her. They were eyes that missed nothing—and at this moment they were fixed with friendly interest on her face.

She smiled widely—she couldn't help it. She hadn't expected to see him again. But this couldn't be the other doctor, could it? She changed her smile to a frown. 'Dr Braden?'

'The very same.' He held out his hand. 'Let's introduce ourselves properly. Dr Kiel Jerome Braden.'

She inclined her head and took his hand, again feeling the strength and warmth of him. 'Teresa Denning.'

'A very welcome addition to our practice. I hope you'll stay longer than the others. You did mention in your letter that you didn't mind moving up here?' He looked her up and down again, as though he couldn't imagine why such a pretty girl should want to bury herself in the country.

Terri felt a stirring in her blood. 'I said that and I meant it,' she returned sincerely. Even more so now she had seen who she was to work with. This man had something about him that she could not quite put a name to, a warmth of personality, a strength of character, a strong sexual magnetism. She wondered how many of his patients fell in love with him. Was that the reason his practice had grown? Her own doctor was nothing like this gorgeous hunk of a man.

'There were reasons you wanted to move?' he enquired smoothly, politely, and yet behind his words was an urgency, a keen desire to know everything.

Terri's voice was cool. 'Personal ones.' She did not see that they were any business of his.

His eyes narrowed. 'So long as it's not to get away from a man. I don't want any irate lover chasing you here.' With mercurial swiftness his tone had changed.

'Nothing like that.' Terri held his gaze, noting how thick and black his lashes were, masking the hardness that had come into his eyes.

She saw no reason to tell him about her broken engagement. Greg was past history. Or Michael West who persistently pursued her even though she had no feelings for him. Besides, he was out of the country at this moment and didn't even know she had moved—or even planned to. Maybe they were a tiny part of the reason she wanted to put London behind her, but not the whole of it.

He nodded, satisfied, and turned towards Barry. 'Barry is my junior partner, as you've obviously discovered. I trust he's been looking after you?'

Junior partner! His statement caused Terri some amusement. There were probably only about six or seven years between them. So much for her image of an old white-haired man who had spent all his life looking after Lakelanders.

'Barry and I have known each other for years,' she answered carefully. 'Actually it's good to see a familiar face. It makes me feel more at home.'

If she thought his attitude had changed before it was nothing compared to the mask of hostility that confronted her now. His velvet-soft growl became clipped and concise, his eyes as hard as the steel colour they were, his mouth grim. 'Why didn't you mention that when you applied?'

Terri felt confused. 'I thought it would look as though I was currying favours, and that was the last——'

'You deliberately kept the truth from me—both of you!' He glared from one to the other. Barry shifted uneasily, casting Terri an apologetic glance. She gave him a tiny wry smile, then looked again at the older man.

'Dr Braden, you have this wrong. Barry didn't even know I'd applied. I assumed he'd told you, once you'd offered me the job, but there's no need to be angry. We didn't cook anything up.'

His head jerked. 'You expect me to believe that? I wouldn't believe anything Barry told me if he swore on a Bible—not where a woman's concerned. It's easy to see what's behind all this.'

Terri could not believe this was the same man. He even looked different. No longer attractive and sensual, his face ugly with anger and accusation, his whole stance rejecting both her and Barry. It didn't make sense.

'I can't see what you're getting at,' she said. And why didn't Barry say something? Why didn't he stick up for her instead of standing there looking distinctly uncomfortable? This man had clearly got things wrong.

The older doctor's eyes narrowed until they were no more than silver slits in his flushed angry face. 'You really thought I wouldn't catch on? What kind of a fool do you take me for, Miss Denning?'

She shook her head, feeling as though she were looking down the twin barrels of a gun. 'I don't know. I mean, you're not a fool—but Barry had nothing to do with me applying for this job. Well, he did tell my brother . . .' Honesty prevailed. 'But he didn't know I would apply. Really he didn't.'

The doctor snorted angrily. 'You're misjudging how well I know Barry. He must have thought he was on to a good thing—a resident nurse willing to fall into his arms—and his bed. No wonder he was in no hurry to move out!'

His icy glare swept over her, right from the top of her heavy blonde hair, down the demure white blouse and ice-blue cotton skirt, to the tips of her feet in neat white sandals. Again she had the sensation that he was undressing her—only this time there was no desire— merely contempt.

'I think the best thing you can do, Miss Denning, is turn right round and go back from where you came. I withdraw my offer of the job.'

Her chin jerked. 'But that's unfair! You can't do that. Barry and I are just friends. You'll have nothing to fear in that respect.'

'And pigs might fly,' he thrust coldly.

'Barry!' She turned to him appealingly. 'For goodness' sake say something. Don't just stand there. Tell him he's made a mistake.'

'Terri's speaking the truth,' said Barry at once. 'You must believe that.'

'Tell him how long we've known each other,' she insisted. 'Why, we're more like brother and sister than anything else.' Why didn't Barry sound convincing? He was no help at all.

'I think Barry is perfectly capable of speaking for himself, Miss Denning,' interjected Kiel Braden drily. 'And the fact that he has nothing to say, unless prompted by you, surely speaks for itself. He's guilty. And so are you. Now go!'

Terri could not believe she was hearing him correctly. What was wrong with the man? Or more to the point, why didn't he trust Barry? Suddenly there came back a forgotten memory of Barry, slightly the worse for drink, making a pass at her on her sixteenth birthday.

She had developed into a beautiful, desirable girl, he had said, was no longer Richard's kid sister, she was grown-up and why didn't they indulge in grown-up pastimes?

Horrified and disgusted, Terri had told him exactly what she thought of him. When they next met he had apologised and the memory had faded so that she had not even thought about it when he hugged her today. It had been seven years ago, after all.

The memory flitted through her mind with the swiftness of a dream and she was unaware that any of her thoughts showed on her face until Dr Braden spat harshly, 'I see I wasn't far off the mark?'

'You're a thousand miles away,' flung Terri, 'and you have no right dismissing me without giving me a fair chance. I'm good at my job, I'm not likely to let you down because I find it too quiet here. Doesn't that count for something?'

Stony eyes bored into her. 'I have no doubt you can do the job standing on your head. Dr Kores spoke highly of you. But I will not be taken for a fool. If you and Barry thought you could get away with it, then you're mistaken.'

'Kiel, for heaven's sake!' Barry suddenly spoke, as though realising Terri's need for support. 'Terri's speaking the truth. There's been no communication between us at all. I haven't seen her for years. And you need her, you know that. It might be ages before you can find anyone to take her place. At least give her a few weeks' trial.'

'Give *you* a few weeks, you mean?' snapped Kiel, fixing his eyes on the younger man.

There was certainly no love lost between them, decided Terri, and wondered what had made Kiel take Barry in with him in the first place. More importantly, she hoped it did not affect their work. Patients needed a calm relaxing atmosphere when visiting their doctor. Tension or friction was the last thing they wanted.

Barry shrugged. 'If that's the way you see it. But I'm thinking of Terri. You're giving her a raw deal. If you turn her away now she'll be out of a job, with not much chance of getting another.'

'She should have thought of that before she decided to chase up here after you,' declared Kiel strongly. 'But you're right, we do need her. You can stay, Miss Denning, but only on a temporary basis, until I can find someone to take your place.' The grey eyes which held her own were as hard and shiny as pebbles on a cold seashore, and about as friendly.

Terri clamped her lips. There was not much she could say that would make him change his mind. All she could do was convince him that he was mistaken, that there was nothing going on between her and Barry, and maybe, just maybe, he would keep her on.

So much for first impressions. The man was nothing at all like the attractive male animal she had thought him. That had simply been a mantle he had assumed for her benefit. This was the real Kiel Braden.

She wondered whether she was expected to say, thank you, that's very generous of you, doctor. Of course she wouldn't. He was doing her no favours, and if the truth were known she would have liked nothing

more than to shoot out of this room and never see him
again.

But a job was a job. Vacancies like this were few and
far between. Once a nurse was established she didn't
often leave. Nurses were a dedicated lot—and if she
had had any inkling of what the situation was here she
would never have given in her notice to Dr Kores.

Since she had she was darned sure she wasn't going
to give up easily. Kiel Braden had no right
condemning *her*, because Barry had given him no
reason to trust *him*.

And it was clear this was the case. Barry had
somehow got himself the title of womaniser—and Dr
Braden thought she was one of his conquests. It would
be her pleasure to prove him wrong. There was
nothing like that between her and Barry. It had been
nipped in the bud many years ago. They both knew
exactly where they stood with each other.

She was glad Barry had spoken up. She had begun
to wonder what was wrong with him. Was he afraid of
Dr Braden? Or was it because he still felt he was on
trial?

Whatever, she had at least got a reprieve and she
was going to make certain that at the end of it all, the
job was still hers. Unless Dr Braden himself made her
life such a misery that she would be glad to leave.
There was always that possibility.

And his next words did nothing to endear him to
her. 'I see now, Barry, why you took your time about
finding yourself somewhere else to live. And you,
Miss Denning——' A sudden malicious smile lifted
the corners of his mouth. 'If what you say is true and
there's nothing going on between you and Barry,
you're in for a shock—since you'll have to share the
flat with him.'

There was a moment's taut silence as he waited for

the full impact of his statement to get through to her. But Terri did not give him the pleasure of seeing that she disliked the idea. She tossed her head and eyed him as coldly as he was viewing her. 'If the flat has two bedrooms I see no problem. I'm used to sharing with a man . . .'

His head jerked, his face growing a dull ugly red, eyes narrowing. 'Miss Denning, I——'

She gave him no chance to put his obvious assumption into words. 'With my brother,' she finished triumphantly. 'And I regard Barry as a brother.'

He was almost spitting fire, and Terri was filled with a desire to laugh. Indeed a chuckle escaped her lips before she pulled herself together. He was so serious it was ridiculous!

Then the telephone shrilled, effectively releasing the tension. Kiel snatched it up, listened attentively, and in a voice that was at complete odds with his earlier whipcord tightness said, 'Barry, Mr Langton's wife's had a fall. You'd best get out to her.'

Barry looked as though he was about to argue, then with a shrug and a helpless look at Terri he collected his case and left.

'You're wrong about Barry and me.' Terri felt compelled to defend herself once they were alone. It was not pleasant staring a job under such conditions.

'Am I?' Brows which were much darker than his blond-streaked hair rose questioningly. His eyes were suddenly pale, but they lost none of their intensity, still impaled her with the sharpness of a surgical instrument.

She nodded. 'Very much so,' and swallowed convulsively. The atmosphere in the room was claustrophobic.

With startling swiftness he caught her wrist in a

biting grip. 'I'd like to think it,' he grated through his teeth. 'In fact it would give me much pleasure to apologise, say I was sorry for thinking the wrong thing.'

'Then why don't you?' she snapped. 'Because it's true. He didn't know I was applying for this job. It wasn't his idea.' His hard-boned fingers were merciless. Terri struggled to free himself, but only succeeded in sending pains shooting up her arm.

She was very conscious of his nearness, of his raw masculinity, of his overpowering aura of sensuality. How could she have thought he had changed, that his hardness had cancelled out his devastating maleness? Nothing, but nothing, would ever annihilate that.

'Are you angry, Teresa?' Steel eyes glittered like molten metal. 'Don't you like what you've heard about your precious boy-friend? Disillusioned, are you? Did you think you'd have him all to yourself? Barry will never be a one-woman man, rest assured about that. The more the merrier as far as he's concerned.'

Her eyes flashed amethyst as she tilted her chin to look at him. He must be at least six foot four, she thought. Six whole feet of simmering, dangerous manhood. 'Our relationship is——'

'I know,' he cut in acidly, 'strictly platonic. Quit the kidology, Teresa. It won't wash with me. I know Barry better than you.'

'How can you,' she cried, 'when I've known him all my life? He was my brother's best friend. He was always in and out of our house at one time. He's practically seen me grow up.'

'And it won't have escaped his notice that you've turned into a beautiful young woman. He never misses an opportunity to make a pass at a pretty girl.' He let go her wrist, but cupped her face instead. 'Especially one with such kissable lips.'

He lowered his head and there was nothing Terri could do to stop him. His hold was invincible. And when he kissed her, she felt she was drowning in a whirlpool of ecstasy. Never had a kiss affected her so abruptly.

It was like nothing she had experienced before. It made every other kiss pallid by comparison, and when he realised she was not fighting, he slid his hands behind her back, holding her against the hard compelling length of him.

Terri knew she ought to struggle, fight, kick, do everything she could to free herself, but it was as though he had taken her over. Instead of resisting, her arms snaked around his neck and she returned his kisses freely, not even stopping to wonder why she was behaving like this with a complete stranger, an enemy even. A man who intended kicking her out of his camp!

It seemed an age before he finally put her from him, even though it could have been no more than a few seconds. His face was inscrutable as he stood looking down at her, awaiting her reaction.

'Why did you do that?' she demanded hotly, snapping to her senses as though she was mechanical and had suddenly been switched on, annoyed more with herself for responding than him for kissing her. What on earth had made her do it?

A slow sardonic smile curved his lips, a light appeared in the steel-grey of his eyes. 'I wanted to find out for myself what sort of a bird my dear brother had invited home to roost. And I think you've given me your answer.'

CHAPTER TWO

'BROTHER?' Terri gazed at Kiel in utter amazement, his kiss forgotten. 'How can Barry Allen be your brother?' Apart from the name difference Barry was an only child.

'My stepbrother, to be exact.' A smile curved his lips and he looked once again the eminently friendly man she had first met. Though she knew now it was all a front, a mask to hide the arrogant aggressive character beneath.

'I didn't know,' she said quickly. 'He's never mentioned you.' She knew Barry's mother had died and his father remarried, but Barry had gone his own way and rarely spoke about them.

'Probably because there's no love lost between us. I have no time for wastrels.'

'Barry isn't that,' she declared stoutly. 'He wouldn't be working here if he was.'

'It wasn't my idea.' With another swift change of mood Kiel's voice grew bitter, his lips grim. 'It's what my mother and stepfather wanted. They thought it might encourage him to settle down.'

Barry wasn't that bad, surely? She cast her mind back. She couldn't remember a lot about him in the early years except that he and Richard had gone around together, and he always seemed a lot of fun. Even when Barry went to university he still came to see them two or three times a year and often regaled them with tales of wild parties. Wine, women and song, he joked, but Terri had seen it as a typical part of student days and not really thought very much about it.

Was he really as bad as Kiel made out? She didn't think so. In fact she refused to believe it. It was this older doctor's word only. Maybe he had a grudge against Barry?

'But he's a qualified doctor,' she argued. 'How can he have wasted his time?'

Kiel snorted derisively. 'He got through by the skin of his teeth. He failed his finals twice, just managed to scrape through the third time. He preferred to spend his time with a girl rather than a textbook. If he was anyone else I wouldn't consider him working with me.' His lips tightened. 'Even now, if he doesn't pull his weight I shall throw him out. And he's going the right way for me to do it.'

Terri drew in a swift angry breath. 'He really didn't know I'd applied. It had nothing to do with him. When are you going to believe that?'

He eyed her hardily. 'I might have been more convinced had you kicked up a fuss when I suggested you and Barry share the flat. You took it with remarkable aplomb—almost as though you were expecting it.'

Terri fumed, feeling on fire. What an infuriating man! How could she have let herself kiss him? Belatedly she wiped the back of her hand across her mouth, and glared. 'I had no choice. Barry is my brother's friend first and foremost. He'll never do anything to offend Richard.'

'I hope you're right.' But the sardonic glint in his eyes told her he meant no such thing. 'It will make a pleasant change seeing my dear brother behave himself. I didn't think he knew how.'

'Then you don't know him all that well,' she snapped.

'Well enough,' he returned, 'and at least he's proving to be a good doctor, which is something. He hasn't let his affairs affect his work—so far.' The look he gave her suggested he'd better not start now—with her!

She tilted her chin. 'I'd be obliged if you'd show me the flat. I'm rather exhausted. I think I'd like to take a rest.'

'In other words, you want to get away from me?'

'Actually, yes,' she returned.

'Am I not what you expected?'

'You're younger,' she said frankly, wondering whether that was humour she saw lurking behind his eyes.

'Is that all?'

'And not so kind and tolerant as a doctor should be,' she added daringly.

'I'm not dealing with a patient.'

Terri inclined her head. 'I'm glad to hear it's not your normal attitude.'

'Barry has a knack of rubbing me up the wrong way.'

She didn't need him to tell her that. 'And because I'm a friend of Barry's you have no time for me either?'

He eyed her gravely. 'I wouldn't exactly say that. I'm prepared to give you the benefit of the doubt—for the time being.' Some of his aggression had gone and Terri felt a resurgence of the instant attraction she had felt at their first meeting.

He took a step closer and she could smell his clean maleness, see the clear grey eyes, feel his magnetic personality. She wanted him to kiss her again, to experience once more those cool lips upon her own, those hands moulding her close to his superbly muscled body. She found she was holding her breath and let out a tiny whisper of disappointment when he stepped past her towards the door.

'I'll carry your cases up. I seem to remember you have quite a few—and it's no task for a woman.' This last was said with a dry smile. He anticipated her response—and got it.

Terri's chin jerked. 'I can manage, thank you. Just show me where I have to go.'

'It's not polite, Teresa, to throw a man's offer back in his face. Or hasn't anyone ever told you that?'

'I'm sorry,' she relaxed. 'I often have to manage things on my own.'

'You've obviously been mixing with the wrong company.'

'Obviously,' she replied, 'and thank you. But I'll still help with the smaller bags. It will save you a few journeys.'

'Stubborn as well as beautiful,' he remarked as he opened the door. 'Quite a combination. I'm even beginning to feel jealous of Barry knowing you all these years and not letting me catch a glimpse of you.'

He had to be joking, but even so a warmth stole through her and there was a smile on her lips as she followed him out to the car.

The flat was reached by a flight of steps on the outside of the building. It was sparsely furnished yet looked reasonably comfortable. There was a living room, a kitchen, two small bedrooms and a shower room.

Kiel carried her luggage through into the spare bedroom, giving her a slightly questioning look before he did so.

Terri said nothing. She was beginning to learn that Kiel would think what he wanted, no matter what anyone said. Only time would convince him that she and Barry were not having an affair.

He left as soon as her things were upstairs. 'The rest of the day is yours,' he said. 'Surgery begins at eight-

thirty in the morning. I'll be here at eight to show you
the ropes.'

After he had gone, the flat felt empty. Not so much
his height or breadth, but the sheer dominant
personality of the man. He took over, he could not be
ignored.

The first thing she did was phone Richard, telling
him about her puncture and the coincidence of Kiel
helping her, but not the remarkable effect he had had,
or even that she would be coming home before long.
She saw no point in spoiling his marital bliss any
earlier than she had to.

She felt hungry, but a search revealed nothing more
than a crust of bread and a hard chunk of cheese.
Obviously Barry did not believe in being well stocked.
He probably ate out—and why shouldn't he?

She toasted the bread and melted the cheese, made a
cup of coffee and sat down. The view from the
window was enchanting. Windermere and the town
were behind her. Here rich green pastures and a
sparkling river crept towards folds of fells, which in
turn climbed steeply towards the sky. Suddenly Terri
was no longer tired. She wanted to explore.

Quickly now she unpacked, took a shower, and
pulled on a pair of jeans and a sleeveless cotton top.
She had never been to the Lakes before and found the
whole district captivating.

Leaving the road, Terri took a well-trodden path
along the valley, coming finally to the river which she
guessed was making its way towards one of the lakes.

The sun caressed her skin, and she sat for a while
on a boulder, her face upturned to its inviting
warmth. She could almost forget she had any worries
about her job.

She spent an hour listening to the incessant drone of
insects, the liquid chirrup of a lark on high, the

whisper of grasses stirred by a breath of wind, the murmur of water chasing its never-ending way across the countryside.

Her thoughts inevitably turned to Kiel. There had been none of the autocrat in him when he stopped to change her wheel. He had regarded her as an interesting and attractive woman, and she had responded.

Now all that had been spoiled. He had kissed her admittedly, but it meant nothing—to him. Whereas she had found it an unforgettable experience. It had woken fires in her that no man had ever kindled before, not even Greg, and quite without realising it she put her fingers to her lips, touching them experimentally.

If she closed her eyes she could still feel the hardness of his mouth, the urgent plundering of her senses. He had no right doing that to her, and yet ironically she was glad he had. It had been like a taste of honey, the sweetness of the man beneath the sometimes stony façade.

There were so many facets to Kiel Braden's nature; he was an enigma, though she knew which side she liked best.

It was with reluctance that Terri eventually retraced her steps and climbed back to the flat. It was oddly quiet. There was no noise of traffic here, no loud honking of horns, or police sirens, or any of the constant hum that was London.

Here you could hear the birds, the faraway bleat of a lamb, the occasional bark of a dog. Apart from that, nothing. She wondered how long Barry would be.

When he finally came in he looked tired, and Terri poured him a cup of coffee from the pot she had kept ready. 'Bad, was it?' she asked.

He nodded. 'Mrs Langton's in hospital—a fractured

femur. Her husband's distraught, refuses to leave. I've been making arrangements for the damn dogs and cats.'

Terri smiled. She couldn't see Dr Kores, or any of the others at the health centre, doing anything like that. But maybe things were different here? Life in the country took on a whole new dimension. She was really looking forward to the change.

Barry drank his coffee and slowly relaxed. 'How long did Kiel stay?'

She shrugged. 'A few minutes.' Long enough for him to kiss her! 'He told me you were stepbrothers. I never realised.'

His mouth twisted wryly. 'We hate each other's guts, that's why. So far as I'm concerned it's unfortunate we both planned to be doctors. I wouldn't work with him from choice.'

'I understand it was your respective parents' idea?'

He inclined his head. 'Whether it works out remains to be seen. I've only been here a few months and I'm not altogether enjoying it.'

'Because of Kiel?'

'Partly,' he frowned. 'But the people are slow to accept me. Kiel's been here a long time, they trust and like him. They're very suspicious of me.' He stood up and paced the room. 'Because I'm newly qualified they seem to think I'm not sure what I'm doing, especially the older ones. I never thought general practice would be like this.'

'Give them time,' smiled Terri. 'I bet Kiel didn't find it easy when he first came. He's not at all like I imagined him to be. I had the biggest shock of my life when I discovered he was the same person who changed my wheel. He doesn't look like my idea of a country doctor.'

'That explains it. I've been wondering how you two had met. What do you think of him?'

Terri grimaced. 'He's a difficult man. I've never known anyone with such swift changes of mood.' But he was also dangerously attractive, though she had no intention of admitting this. 'Is that the reason he's never married?'

Barry shrugged. 'He's had plenty of girls, but his work always come first, and none of them fancy playing second fiddle. I honestly don't know why he remains a G.P. He's extremely interested in nutrition. He ought to stick solely to that.'

This did not surprise Terri. He struck her as the type of man to climb mountains. She could not see him remaining in this one job for the rest of his life. Something much higher, more demanding, was surely his line? She would have liked to question Barry more deeply about Kiel but was afraid to give away her interest in him.

'How about you?' she asked instead. 'Have you any ambitions?'

'To have a good time,' he grinned. 'Though there's not much chance of that in this dead-and-alive hole. I sometimes think it's why my mother insisted I join forces with Kiel. She didn't approve of my—er—lifestyle.'

'So it's true, what Kiel says about you?' Terri asked in a shocked voice.

'What's that?' He was suddenly wary.

'That you have a reputation where girls are concerned. I was horrified when he said it had taken you three attempts to pass your exams. Now I can see why. Shame on you, Barry! I take back my earlier congratulations.'

He grinned unconcernedly. 'Now you've discovered my secret vices have you changed your opinion of me?' His face was very close.

Terri laughed and shook her head. 'You're still like

a brother to me, nothing will alter that.'

But the look he suddenly gave her was not that of a brother, but a man who is interested in a woman for an entirely different reason. She looked uneasily away.

'Put your glad rags on,' said Barry, not seeming to notice anything wrong. 'I know a place about five miles from here where they serve a delicious steak.'

Terri needed no persuading, pushing to the back of her mind her sudden new and disquieting thoughts. Barry liked girls, yes. What healthy virile male didn't? She was mistaken in thinking he regarded her in any other light than that of a friend. She was being over-imaginative, that was all.

She changed into a soft green sundress with a matching jacket, brushed her thick, silken hair into a smooth curtain about her face, and pronounced herself ready. She intended enjoying every moment of this evening. Her day had been spoilt. Her job was in jeopardy, and she dared not think about the future. So why not make the most of her opportunities?

The restaurant was on the shore of a lake and their table situated in the window overlooking the still waters which mirrored to perfection the trees and hills on the opposite bank.

A red-sailed yacht glided gracefully past. It was incredibly peaceful and beautiful, making Terri feel that time stood still, that life was passing them by, ignoring their existence.

The Lakes, she was quickly discovering, were a place apart. You could lose all sense of time, feel none of the pressures of normal everyday life. It was an experience. Something she had never felt before. She had always been so much a part of a busy community that she had never known places like this existed.

'Penny for them?' Barry's voice cut into her thoughts.

Terri brought herself back with a start. 'I'm getting the feel of my surroundings. I've never been anywhere so tranquil.'

'It can also be boring.' Barry did not look so enthusiastic. 'You should be here in winter.'

'I bet it's out of this world,' said Terri at once. 'I can imagine all these fells covered in snow, the lake frozen. It must look like a miniature Switzerland.'

'And as dead as a dodo,' put in Barry glumly. 'Some of the roads become impassable. You can be cut off for days. It's no fun then, I assure you.'

'Because you'd still have to get out if anyone was sick? Mm, I hadn't thought of that. How often do you get a night off? I suppose one of you has to be on call.'

'The telephone's switched through to Kiel's house,' he informed her, 'but it's a flexible system.' He patted his pocket. 'I carry a bleeper around and you can bet your bottom dollar he always disturbs me when I'm enjoying myself. Talk of the devil, guess who's just walked in?'

Terri glanced across and caught her breath. Kiel had changed into an immaculate beige suit with a brown and white striped shirt. He looked taller than ever, easily the most striking man in the room.

As if he already knew they were there he came straight towards them. His loose-limbed confident stride reminded Terry of a predatory animal—and she had the uneasy feeling that she was his quarry.

But she fixed a smile to her lips and looked up at him. The grey unfathomable eyes were riveted upon her, his tawny hair swept tidily across his forehead. A quiver ran through her and she cursed herself for responding when he had such a low opinion of her. There was something about him, though, that she found difficult to ignore, and her awareness grew instead of diminishing.

B

'I knew this was where I'd find you,' he said pleasantly. 'Barry brings all his girlfriends here.'

'You mean you're spying on us?' Barry sounded irritable.

Kiel lifted his broad shoulders indifferently. 'My housekeeper wasn't expecting me back and didn't bother cooking, so I thought I'd eat here. Do you mind if I join you?'

'Yes, I do damn well mind,' exploded Barry. 'It's been a long time since I saw Terri. I'd like some time alone with her.'

'The night is young,' replied Kiel evenly. 'Don't worry. I have no intention of burdening you with my company for the whole evening.'

But for long enough, thought Terri. Her heartbeats had quickened annoyingly and she knew she would not enjoy her food with him at her side. He was by far the sexiest male animal she had ever met, drawing out a response in her whether she liked it or not.

Heedless of the fact that neither of them wanted him, Kiel signalled the waiter to bring an extra chair, and within seconds a place had been set and he was studying the menu.

It was an uncomfortable meal. Kiel insisted on monopolising the conversation, talking about various cases to Barry, things about which Terri knew nothing. She felt sure he was deliberately excluding her from the conversation, anything to make her feel awkward.

They ordered coffee and then Kiel's pager bleeped. 'Excuse me,' he said. 'My housekeeper. This always happens when you least want it.' His eyes rested on Terri for a long second—then he was gone.

'Thank goodness for that,' said Barry. 'He won't come back. He always puts his work first. He has a passion for it that's unbelievable.'

'Do you really think he knew we'd be here?' asked Terri, 'or was it coincidence?'

'It was no coincidence,' he assured her. 'It was his intention to spoil our evening. If he had his way you'd be on your way back to London now. He doesn't trust me one inch.'

'Well, at least we're rid of him.' Without thinking Terri put her hand across the table to cover Barry's, and it was too late to retract it when he raised it to his lips in a gallant gesture.

'I wish I'd never mentioned this job to Richard. I'm sorry if things aren't turning out as you expected.'

'It's not your fault,' she said quickly. 'You didn't know how he'd react. I wish he'd believed me, though. It's not nice being called a liar.'

'I'm sorry to break up this intimate little scene.' Kiel had returned without either of them noticing. 'But you're wanted, Barry. Laura Monk. She asked for you particularly. Her mother's having another asthma attack.'

'Why can't you go?' asked Barry belligerently. 'I can't leave Terri, it's not fair on her.'

Kiel's eyes narrowed. 'Has Laura lost her attraction now there's another girl in your life?' His eyes flicked over Terri damningly. 'Perhaps I ought to warn you that Barry's affections blow like the wind.'

'I resent that remark!' Barry thrust his jaw aggressively, looking as though he would like to floor Kiel with a punch.

'I think you ought to go,' said Terri worriedly.

Kiel nodded. 'I'll look after Terri. She'll be quite safe with me.'

'Safe, yes, but happy? You've already upset her.' He held determinedly on to Terri's hand. 'You're being unfair, Kiel.'

'Am I?' The grey eyes were rock-hard. 'Get your

skates on, Barry. You're going whether you like it or not.'

With great reluctance Barry let her go and stood up, his lips compressed, holding back his anger with difficulty. 'I'll see you at the flat, Terri. I shouldn't be long.'

'Take your time,' said Kiel lightly. 'Don't worry about Terri.'

'But I am worried about her. I've been trying to make her evening pleasant after the shock of finding herself without a proper job.'

Kiel's smile held no humour. 'I'll do my best to carry on your good work.'

Barry frowned, seemed about to say something else, then stopped, swinging on his heel and marching from the restaurant.

Kiel slid back on his seat and poured himself a cup of coffee from the pot that had arrived in his absence. Terri felt like kicking his shins beneath the table. He had done this deliberately!

'I'm sorry Barry had to leave. It's one of the pitfalls of the job, being called out unexpectedly.' His voice held no trace of the anger that had sharpened it earlier.

'You could have gone yourself.' Terri felt cross and ungracious and would have liked more than anything to walk out. Kiel was being annoyingly pleasant about the whole incident, and there was no doubt in her mind that he had deliberately got rid of Barry.

'Barry's gone willingly to see Mrs Monk on other occasions,' he said. 'You're making a pretty bad show of pretending there's nothing between you.'

'There isn't!' She raised her eyes to his face and discovered him watching her from beneath lowered lids. An instant charge of electricity ran through her limbs and she almost felt it was a pity circumstances were such as they were. A deeper relationship could have been very rewarding. Even the mere thought of it made her head spin.

But there was no chance of anything like that happening. He resented her presence and she couldn't think why he had burdened himself with her tonight. No, she did know why. He had done it to spite his stepbrother, but certainly not because he wanted her company.

'I think you treat Barry very harshly,' she said.

Kiel's smile was wry. 'He needs a firm hand. You think you know him, but you don't. You've seen only his good side.'

'I don't believe he has a bad one,' snapped Terri, deliberately pushing aside her few disquieting thoughts. 'He likes girls, okay, so what man doesn't? Are you trying to tell me that you're a celibate? That you live for your work, devoting your entire life to it?'

He grimaced cynically. 'I'm not saying that at all. I enjoy a woman's company, but there's a time and place for everything. That's what Barry doesn't seem to realise. One day he'll settle down, I suppose, but he's taking a hell of a long time about it.'

Terri drank her coffee, glaring coldly over the rim of her cup. Then she pushed back her chair. 'I'd like to go now, if you wouldn't mind.'

'But I do mind,' said Kiel. 'I got rid of Barry so that I could have your company for an hour or two.'

Her eyes shot wide, they had never been more brilliantly purple. 'What for? So that you can tell me again what a fool I am for thinking I could pull the wool over your eyes? Aren't you ever going to believe that I told the truth, that Barry means nothing more than a friend to me and never has?'

His brows slid up. 'It didn't look like that to me just now. You were holding hands and looking into each other's eyes as only lovers can. Are you trying to tell me that it was entirely innocent?'

'Yes, it was,' cried Terri, alarmed to feel hot colour flooding her cheeks. She had never told a lie in her life. 'We're friends, that's all.'

'Barry couldn't be friends, pure platonic friends, with a woman if he tried.'

Terri was beginning to believe this, but she was blowed if she would say as much to Kiel. 'You're wrong—very wrong. And I'm not going to stay here and listen to your insinuations a moment longer. If you won't take me then I'll call a taxi. Good night, Dr Braden!'

She stood up, angrily swinging around, unaware that her bag was in a direct line with Kiel's cup. The first she knew about it was his cry of rage when hot coffee spilt down his shirt front.

'Why, you clumsy little fool!' he gritted through his teeth.

'Oh, Lord, I'm sorry,' said Terri, aghast. 'I didn't mean to do that, honestly. Here, let me mop it up.' She grabbed a napkin, but he knocked her hand away savagely.

'We shall have to go now but you're coming back to my place. I refuse to sit in these wet clothes while I run you home.'

Terri's heart fell and she wished she had been more careful. She had wanted to get away from this annoyingly attractive man, now she had to spend even more time with him.

It was a chastened Terri who followed Kiel out to his car, and neither spoke as they hurtled through the night. Very faintly came the odour of Kiel's aftershave, but stronger was the smell of coffee, and she chastised herself again for her carelessness.

A crescent moon hung over the distant fells, stars

gave a faint display of promised brilliance. Terri was
awed by the peace of it all, and had it not been for Kiel
using the road as a race track she would have enjoyed
this short moment between daylight and the velvet
cloak of darkness.

They shot past the long deserted shores of a silent
lake; no breeze stirred the leaves of the trees, or
rippled the surface of the water. Terri would have
liked to stop, to look and listen, but dared not ask.

As it grew darker, pinpoints of light appeared on the
far shore, reflected in long silver streaks across the
lake. The mountains merged as one with the sky and
Kiel swung the car off the road and began to climb.

His headlights pierced the darkness like laser beams.
They climbed for what seemed like several hundred
feet before he charged between two stone pillars and
along a winding tree-lined drive. His house was set
high on the top of a hill. A stately home that looked
more like a mansion than anything else. Lights shone
out from a downstairs window, spilling welcoming
yellow warmth.

The car screeched to a halt and he got out,
unfolding his long length. Terri followed suit, but
more slowly, and stood for a moment looking about
her. She imagined that during daylight the views here
would be superb, but tonight she could see nothing.

An owl hooted forlornly in trees silhouetted blackly
against the dark sky. A nightjar called. Something
stirred in the undergrowth. Distant lights looked like
stars that had fallen down out of the sky.

She felt sad that this could possibly be her one and
only visit to this house and turned hurriedly as Kiel
called her from the entrance. 'It's beautiful,' she said
involuntarily. 'You must love living here.'

'It suffices,' he said brusquely, and led the way
inside.

The hall was vast and square with polished parquet flooring and Chinese rugs. The walls were covered with satin embossed wallpaper in palest green. A crystal chandelier shimmered above their heads, and plants cascaded from urns and pots.

Kiel opened a door and ushered her into a surprisingly small and cosy room. In one corner stood a desk with a studded leather chair in front of it. There were easy chairs and a Persian carpet, and lovingly cared for antiques.

'If you'll wait here,' he said, 'I'll shower and change. Help yourself to a drink.'

A crystal decanter stood on a low carved table, a single glass beside it. Terri guessed it was meant for him, but poured herself a small measure of whisky, topping it with water from a matching crystal jug.

In ten minutes he was back. Gone was the suit and coffee-stained shirt, replaced with a pair of slate-grey corduroy trousers and a fine-knit casual shirt.

His hair looked darker now it was wet, all one colour instead of the several shades of blond that gave it its tawny appearance. He looked more vitally masculine, if that were possible, and Terri drew in a swift silent breath, watching as he opened a cupboard and selected another glass, pouring himself a drink before coming to stand near the armchair where she sat.

He held the glass up in mocking salute, but said nothing as he took his first sip. He simply stood and looked down at her, an enigmatic smile briefly curving his lips.

Terri would have given anything to know what he was thinking. 'You have a nice house,' she said, feeling a need to break the silence. 'Do your parents live here?'

He shook his head, his smile widening. 'I'm a little old to be living under my mother's wing. I bought this place a couple of years ago. It's my bolt-hole. No one comes here unless invited.'

'Then I suppose I'm honoured?' asked Terri.

His brows rose mockingly. 'I had no choice.'

'And how many girls have you brought here?' Terri did not know why she asked this question, except that somehow it seemed important.

He surprised her. 'None. I like my privacy. There's just me and my housekeeper and that suits me very well.'

'Where is she now?'

He grinned. 'Gone to bed, I expect. We're as good as alone.'

Terri felt momentary panic, and it was there in her eyes for him to see.

'Scares you, does it? Afraid I might take advantage? Let's say I never force myself on anyone. My partner has to be willing.'

Although the assurance was a relief, Terri knew that should he attempt to kiss her she would be more than willing, her attraction was growing by the minute, which was stupid, considering his opinion of her. He thought she was as free with her love as Barry.

CHAPTER THREE

'By the way, did you get your puncture repaired?' With a swift and unexpected change of subject Kiel broke the moment of tension.

Terri shook her head, finding it difficult to drag her mind back to practicalities. One second he had been looking at her with fire in his eyes, the next—nothing.

'Then see to it without delay. The Lakes are no place to be stranded without a spare. Would you like to have a look around the house?'

Again another abrupt topic change, one which set alarm bells jangling in her head. She looked at him, startled, but his expression did not suggest that there was any ulterior motive behind his invitation. Besides, his housekeeper was about somewhere. She only had to scream should he prove troublesome. 'I'd love to,' she said. 'I just wish it were daylight. I bet the views from up here are fantastic.'

He looked pleased by her enthusiasm as he led the way out of the room. She was impressed by his well-stocked library, the elegant drawing-room and stately dining-room. There was a large lounge and a conservatory. Another room held nothing but a grand piano, and she wondered whether he played. And the kitchen was a dream of electronic gadgetry.

She hadn't expected him to show her upstairs, especially with his housekeeper in bed, and she felt surprised and a little hesitant when he began to climb the wide shallow steps. But after a second's pause she followed, feeling instinctively that she could trust him.

It was herself she did not trust.

The stairs creaked beneath their weight. It was an old house, yet well looked after and comfortable. Terri felt it had been a happy house and envied Kiel living here.

There was a galleried landing and all the rooms were tastefully furnished, some with their own private bathrooms. 'Mrs Barnes',' he said in a hushed voice, indicating one of the doors, 'and mine,' he added later, casting her a wicked glance as he did so.

She felt oddly disappointed that he did not show her inside. A person's bedroom reflected their character and she imagined this would be as neat and tidy as his consulting room, probably as clinical too. He struck her as the type who had a place for everything and there was hell to pay if it wasn't kept there.

Back downstairs he refilled her glass. 'So what's your opinion of my modest home now?'

'I'd hardly call it modest,' smiled Terri. 'It's the nicest home I've ever been in. It's not what I expected, though, for a G.P. How can you afford to run it?' She hoped he wouldn't consider her impertinent, but after all he had been showing off, and it was far grander than any of the houses the doctors at the health centre owned. It was only the consultants and surgeons who could afford places such as this.

He shrugged. 'I've written several very successful books on nutrition. I conduct a radio question time. I hold occasional seminars, and so forth. It's all very lucrative stuff.'

'So why the practice as well?'

'Because,' he smiled, 'I like to keep in touch. It's surprising what you learn from ordinary everyday folk. Sit down, I feel like some company.'

Terri swallowed hard, alarmed to feel her heartbeats accelerating. 'I'd rather go.' She did not think it wise to stay much longer. Besides, Barry would wonder what had happened to her.

'You mean you still don't trust me?' There was a dangerous darkening to his eyes.

'I don't know what to think,' husked Terri, wondering if he could hear her heart.

'Then I'll tell you what you're thinking.' His voice hardened. 'You're attracted to me, but because I've refused you the job you're trying to hate me.' He caught the tell-tale flicker in her eyes. 'And I'll be honest with you, you're a very attractive woman yourself. In other circumstances I might feel differently about you. As things are I see you as nothing but one of Barry's cheap little friends. You probably turn to any man who pays you the slightest attention.'

Terri flinched as though he had struck her. 'I don't think I asked for that! You're wrong, very wrong.' She felt sick inside and blamed her stupidity in responding to his kiss earlier. It had given him entirely the wrong impression. 'I never knew Barry was—like you say. I don't even believe you. But I shan't hang around him. I want this job, I really do. Can't you see it from my point of view?'

'Are you pleading with me?' Kiel sounded amused, but Terri did not find it funny.

'I wouldn't plead with you,' she snapped, 'not even if it meant I was out of a job and a home. I'm just trying to appeal to your better nature—if you have one?'

'In business one has to learn never to let one's heart rule one's head,' said Kiel smoothly. 'In that way you never regret a decision. Allowing you to stay indefinitely might prove a disastrous mistake.'

'God, you're heartless!' she cried. 'Completely and utterly heartless. I can't imagine how you ever managed to become a doctor. You don't care about people at all. It's easy to see why you're not married. I doubt anyone would be able to put up with your— insults!'

His brows slid upwards. 'Do go on, I find this most interesting.'

'You can mock,' she flung at him, heedless of the sleeping woman upstairs, 'but it's true! Every single word of it. I'm not surprised Barry hates your guts, and perhaps I shall be better off out of it. I can see the next few days are going to be miserable. Can I go back to the flat now?'

'When I'm good and ready,' he drawled. 'You're intriguing me. You're quite a spitfire when you get going. I expect Barry finds you hard to handle. I'm beginning to wonder whether it wasn't you who cajoled him into finding you a job, not the other way round as I first thought.'

Terri's eyes were blazing by the time he had finished, her face alight with anger. 'If that's what you want to think, it's your prerogative, but if I were Barry I wouldn't stick it here for one minute. You're impossible!'

He smiled, as though he found her indignation highly entertaining. 'Barry has no choice, not at the moment. Once he's settled, I see no reason why he shouldn't join some other practice. As he is, no one would entertain him. His only redeeming factor is that his private life doesn't affect his work.'

'And so you have a dig at him at every possible opportunity, instead of guiding and advising?'

Kiel sighed deeply and impatiently. 'You don't know the half. You've only seen the good side of Barry—which I admit is pretty attractive—to a woman. If you knew him as I do you'd realise what he's really like.'

'I'm not here to discuss Barry,' she said tightly, 'and I don't see why you should inflict your opinions on me. I make up my own mind, thank you. I've never found him anything but charming and friendly.' She felt she was entitled to a tiny white lie. One minor incident seven years ago was not worth mentioning.

'God dammit, woman, you're so unreasonable!' He gave a snort of anger and turned away. 'The sun shines out of his eyes so far as you're concerned. You'll be in for a rude awakening one of these days.' The air was filled with a crackling tension and his eyes were frostily cold as he looked at her.

Consumed with a boiling anger, Terri crossed to the door. 'If all you're going to do is shoot Barry down, then I see no point in remaining.' She held her chin high, aware of how frail she was compared to this big man, swinging the door wide and looking at him bravely. 'I'd like to go—now.'

'To an empty flat?' he demanded bitterly, his face sharply angular. 'Barry won't be back for hours— Laura will see to that. You might just as well stay.'

'And listen to you running both him and me down? No, thank you. I prefer my own company.' Which was not strictly true, because she hated to be alone. She did not particularly like large crowds, but she did like one or two people with her.

If things had been different she would have willingly waited here a while longer. It was such a magnificent house. She loved anything that was beautiful and luxurious, and this certainly fitted the bill.

'I won't mention him again,' Kiel said unexpectedly, 'although I imagine you'll have difficulty in pushing him from your mind, considering he's the main reason you're here.'

Terri shook her head wildly, silken hair flying. 'For the last time, Barry means nothing to me—not in the way you're insinuating.' Why, oh, why couldn't he accept that?

His brows rose cynically. 'It's not how I saw things earlier. You had eyes only for each other.' He came towards her, closed the door, put his hand on her back and propelled her towards the chair.

His touch was light, almost non-existent, yet it seared Terri as though he were using a red-hot iron. She wondered what it was about him that was getting beneath her skin, and almost wished she had never seen this charming side. She could then have hated him as he deserved.

Reluctantly she sat down, picking up the drink she had abandoned earlier. Kiel slotted a tape into a recorder and music filled the room. Terri leaned back and closed her eyes, allowing the haunting melody to wash over her. Gradually some of her tension went and she almost forgot that the hateful Dr Braden was in the room with her.

But when she opened her eyes he was there all right, sitting opposite, his steely gaze fixed on her, almost as though he was trying to commit her face to memory.

She glanced at him stonily. 'So now you've got me to stay what are we going to talk about?'

'You?' he suggested lightly. 'Tell me about yourself. I know nothing except that you're a friend of my stepbrother.'

'Correction,' hissed Terri. 'My brother is Barry's friend. But I thought we'd agreed not to talk about him?'

'It's difficult to leave him out of the conversation,' he said heavily, 'but I'll try. Is Richard your only brother? Have you any sisters?'

'Just Richard,' she said.

'And your parents are dead, I believe? That horrific plane crash a couple of years ago in Spain.'

Terri's head jerked. 'How do you know that?'

He lifted his broad shoulders lazily. 'I felt it my duty to check up on why you were applying for a job so far away from home. Dr Kores was most obliging—said how distraught you'd been since their death. He could understand you wanting to move away.'

'How dare you!' Terri was incensed, standing abruptly, fixing her eyes angrily on his face. 'My private life has nothing at all to do with you.' He had taken a liberty, discussing her like this with Dr Kores. All that need have concerned him was her ability as a nurse, nothing else. Her whole body vibrated with fury.

'I have to safeguard my own interests,' he said mildly, unconcerned by her anger.

Maybe he did, but why go behind her back? 'What else did you ask him?'

He looked at her long and hard. 'As a matter of fact I enquired whether you had a boy-friend. I wanted no trouble in that quarter, as I've already mentioned. He didn't know. Obviously you kept Barry a closely guarded secret.'

Terri sent him a savage, smouldering glance. 'It's not worth arguing with you. Please take me back to the flat. And this time I mean it. I don't want to stay with you a moment longer.'

She didn't care that she was stepping out of line, that he could quite easily tell her to pack her bags and leave altogether. He really was insufferable!

And thank goodness Dr Kores had not known about her brief disastrous engagement. That really would have given Kiel Braden some ammunition to fire. She had met Greg just after her parents' death, when she wasn't really thinking straight. Fortunately it had been a mutual decision to break the engagement, and there had been no hard feelings on either side.

Since then she had had no regular boy-friend, unless she counted the persevering Michael. He was more a nuisance than anything else. He was their next-door neighbour. They had gone to school together and grown up together, and he seemed to think this gave him some prior claim. But she would never love Michael. Like Barry, he was no more than a friend.

Kiel's lips were grim as he hauled himself up, and there was bitter silence between them as he drove with maniacal speed through the night.

The flat was in darkness and Terri shivered inwardly. She did not mind the dark, when it was somewhere familiar, but here it was strange and hostile and she knew she would not rest until Barry came home.

But surprisingly Kiel got out of the car too and followed her up the stone steps. He pulled a key out of his pocket and opened the door, snapping on the light and going in first. Terri was not sure she liked the idea of Kiel having a key, even though the property belonged to him. It meant he could walk in at any time.

'I'll be all right now,' she said, and then jumped as the phone rang.

'You look mighty nervous to me,' he grated, and as the phone continued to shrill, 'Hadn't you better answer that?'

She shook her head. 'It won't be for me.'

He looked impatient. 'Answer it.'

Terri took a deep breath and lifted the receiver. It was a relief to hear Barry's voice. 'I'm glad you're back,' he said. 'Trust that stepbrother of mine to ruin the evening! I won't be home for a couple of hours yet, so don't wait up.' A pause, then, 'You are all right?'

'Of course,' said Terri quickly. 'I'm so tired I shall probably fall asleep before my head touches the pillow. I'll see you in the morning.'

'He's not coming home yet? I guessed it.' Kiel's comments were harshly sneeringly cynical, his lips curled in contempt.

'If you knew this would happen why did you send him?' she demanded aggressively, wondering how you could hate a person and yet feel physically excited at the same time. She had heard it said it was easier to hate than love, how true this was proving.

'Can't you guess?' The grey eyes were alight with mockery. 'I wanted you to see him in his true light. Now do you believe that you're not the only girl in his life?'

'I never was,' she snapped.

'So you knew you were just one of a crowd?' Brows rose questioningly. 'Available whenever he felt like coming to see you?'

Terri drew in a deep shuddering breath. 'God, I hate you!' Her eyes flashed purple.

Kiel smiled slowly, white teeth gleaming, and his hands fell on her shoulders. She felt the heat emanating from his body, a fierce sensual heat that enflamed her senses. 'I'm doing you a favour, Teresa, turning you away from here.'

As he spoke he lowered his head and suddenly she found herself clasped tightly in his arms, his mouth devouring hers. Quite how it happened she was not sure, but there was a hunger in him as he ravaged her lips, an ardour that could not be denied.

At first she struggled, but then, as a whole host of fiery emotions were released, she returned his kisses eagerly. He drugged her. He made her unaccountable for her actions, he filled her with aching desire.

And yet all he was trying to do was prove that she

and Barry were not suited. He was not kissing her because he wanted to. He despised her. This was an exercise—and she ought to fight, to resist, to at least put up some show of self-defence.

But somehow her mind refused to accept what she knew to be true. She wanted him to kiss her, for whatever reason. She enjoyed it. It was a sensation that outstripped all sensations.

It was fortunate, though, that she would not be here long, for how could she face him with something like this between them? How could she work for him and not feel this desire?

Her head spun as his kiss deepened, his hands exploring her back, sliding up to embrace her head, strong fingers mingling in her hair, imprisoning her so that there was no escape even had she wanted to— which she didn't. Her lips parted involuntarily, accepting his deep urgent kisses, pressing her body close, feeling the vibrating, pulsing strength of him.

It seemed an eternity before he finally let her go. A whole lifetime of being held in his arms and made to feel that he desired her, found her irresistible. It was difficult to believe that he was doing it deliberately to prove a point—or that she had only met him that day! This was the most amazing part of all. It was almost as though they were—meant for each other.

Weakened, Terri groped for a chair. There was a smile in his eyes. 'Barry doesn't know what he's missing. I'm quite sure Laura isn't a patch on you. If you don't mind me saying so, you're a fool throwing your life away on him.'

'I'm a fool to let you kiss me,' she cried—and an even bigger idiot to let him see that she enjoyed it!

'It was a pleasant experience,' he admitted, 'but I'm not quite sure what you were trying to achieve. It told me in no uncertain terms that you're no more faithful to Barry than he is you. It also makes me wonder whether you weren't hoping that by responding to me it might change my mind about sending you away.'

Terri backed, her eyes wide with shock. 'I'd never sell myself to a man. What I did was involuntary. Much as it sickens me to admit this, you're a very attractive man, Dr Braden. Although I'm sure you don't need me to tell you that!'

'I don't usually have any trouble,' he confessed, smiling drily.

'You mean girls throw themselves into your arms?' Like she had, damn it!

His eyes glinted. 'It has been known.'

'And you wouldn't hurt their feelings by rejecting them?' What a conceited swine he was!

He did not miss the sarcasm in her voice. 'Why refused what's offered?'

'Why indeed?' she said, turning away, feigning a yawn. 'I'd like to go to bed now, if you wouldn't mind. There's no point in waiting up for Barry.'

'None at all,' he agreed pleasantly, 'but are you sure you're not simply trying to get rid of me because you're disturbed by the depth of your feelings? Or do you respond like that to any man who chooses to kiss you?'

There was an ominous glitter in his eyes and Terri held his gaze for a fraction of a second before looking away. He saw too much for her peace of mind.

Nor could she understand her reaction. It was as though she had no control over her body. Her mind warred, yet her response had been unconscious. 'Your kiss meant nothing to me at all,' she said distantly, 'and it's actually the first time I've ever kissed a man I—I *despise*.'

He looked sceptical, brows rising briefly, grey eyes wide and clear. 'A strong word, Miss Denning. I should make sure you mean it.' He moved to the door. 'Pleasant dreams, and don't be late in the morning.'

The door closed and she was left with a feeling of relief. It had been quite an eventful evening. So much so that she doubted whether she would sleep, even though she had told Kiel she was tired.

She felt ashamed by the wantonness of her kiss and could not even recall responding to Greg with so much enthusiasm.

Her reflection in the bedroom mirror did not help. Her eyes were unusually bright, her mouth soft and red with that just-kissed look, her hair wild. She ripped off her clothes and ran into the shower room, standing for long minutes beneath the cleansing jets, hating herself for the way she had behaved. It was no wonder he thought she was as bad as Barry!

Eventually she went to bed, but not to sleep. The blackness and silence which seemed to close in all about her was scary. At home she was used to the light from the street lamps filling her bedroom, the sound of traffic, and the confidence that her brother was asleep in the same house.

Here there was no one. She was in the middle of nowhere and every sound, every slight creak the old building made, was new to her. She wished Barry would hurry back. Sleep was impossible. Not only was there the strangeness, the suffocating silence, but her disturbing thoughts about Kiel. The combination was powerful.

She must have been in bed an hour when the strident ring of the telephone crashed into the silence, startling her, causing her heartbeats to quicken. She switched on the light and went through into the other room. It could only be Barry—perhaps to say that he had been detained even longer?

'Is that you, Barry?' she asked, as she snatched up the receiver, her voice high and jerky.

'Sorry to disappoint you,' came a velvet-soft growl. 'But at least it's given me the answer to my question.'

'Kiel!' There was a further frantic quickening of her heart. 'What do you want?'

'To make sure you're all right. That my erring stepbrother has returned to look after you.'

'Now you know he hasn't,' she snapped. 'But you needn't have checked, I'm fine.'

'You don't sound it,' he returned tersely. 'In fact I'd say you're extremely nervous. It would be no trouble at all for me to come back and keep you company.'

No trouble! Who was he kidding? It was the last thing she wanted. Her equilibrium had only just returned to normal. 'No, no,' she said, 'don't put yourself out. I'm all right, perfectly all right.' And she was also speaking too quickly, giving herself away despite her brave words.

'I'm simply thinking of you,' he said smoothly. 'There's no need to bite my head off.'

'You knew I'd be in bed,' she accused.

'But were you asleep?'

She paused, then said reluctantly, 'No, I wasn't. Not that I'm afraid, or anything like that. It's just so quiet. I'm not used to it.'

'The Lakes are like that,' he said softly. 'It's really the most peaceful place on earth. But you should try to get some sleep or you won't be fit for work tomorrow.'

And that was all he cared about! 'Don't worry,' she bit, 'I shall cope. I shan't let you down.'

'Good. Now I'll let you go back to bed.'

'Thanks for ringing,' she said ungraciously, and put down the phone. He had known she would be unable to sleep, damn him! He was as aware of the effect he had on her as she was herself. But he had no right disrupting her life. What could he possibly hope to gain?

Knowing it would be impossible to sleep now, Terri boiled the kettle and made herself a cup of tea. Hot milk might have been more soothing, but since there was only powdered milk, tea had to do.

She took it through to the sitting-room, sipping slowly, her thoughts on Kiel. She had almost finished when she heard footsteps outside. They paused at the top of the steps and she held her breath. Then a key was inserted and turned in the lock, and relief flooded over her. An intruder wouldn't have a key. It was Barry at last.

But it was Kiel who stepped into the room. Her eyes widened at the sight of him. 'Why are you here?' She was conscious that her short cotton nightie exposed almost the full length of her legs, and scarcely hid anything else.

'I tried to ring Barry, to tell him to get a move on. He wasn't there, would you believe? He's taken Laura out. Lord knows what time he'll be back. You sounded nervous—I thought you needed protection.'

'Not by you,' she flung angrily. If the truth were known she needed protection *from* him.

'It's all right,' he said calmly, soothingly. 'You can go to bed. I'll just sit here and wait until Barry returns. That way you'll be able to relax.'

With him outside her door? He had to be joking. 'It's very thoughtful of you, but not necessary.' Her voice was tight and she was appalled to feel a tingling awareness run through her. The situation was unreal, and certainly something she had not envisaged when setting out from home that morning.

'I know what it's like to be in a strange place,' he returned evenly. 'Whenever I go away I can never sleep the first night. It's not like your own bed, is it? But you really should try to get some sleep.'

'It's not exactly that,' she replied tightly. 'It's you! There's no way I'll be able to sleep with you sitting out here. You made a mistake thinking it would help. I'd rather you went.'

'You mean ...' His eyes glinted dangerously. 'You're afraid I might take advantage? If you knew me better, Teresa, you'd realise that's not my style. You have my word that I'll not enter your bedroom.'

Terri set down her cup which she had been clutching like a lifeline and stood up. 'I don't seem to have much choice. When you make up your mind you never change it, do you? That much I've learned.'

He stood in a direct line between her and the bedroom door, and Terri was vitally aware of her state of semi-nudity, feeling the power of his eyes as they appraised her.

Some devil inside made her halt in front of him, tilting her head defiantly so that she could look up into his eyes, heedless that she was dicing with danger. 'Good night, Dr Braden, I'm flattered that you took the trouble to come. It was very kind of you.'

There was a moment's breathless silence as he weighed up whether she meant it or not, then he put one finger beneath her chin. 'It's my pleasure.'

Terri was suddenly immobilised, unable to repress the quivers of sensation his gentle touch evoked. Then the door burst open and Barry charged into the room, taking in the situation at a glance. 'What the devil do you think you're doing? Get away from Terri at once!'

She felt as guilty as if they had been caught in the act of making love. Kiel, on the other hand, looked at Barry coolly, his face expressionless. 'If you'd had the decency to look after your friend there'd have been no need for me to be here. She was afraid, on her own.'

'I doubt you gave her chance to be that,' snarled Barry, his face an ugly mask. 'It looks as though I got here just in time!'

'It's not what it looks like,' Terri interrupted, not wanting these two men to argue over her. 'Kiel hasn't been here all night. He came back when he discovered I was still alone.'

'You invited him, dressed like that?' Barry looked as though he was about to explode, his face red and outraged, bouncing on the balls of his feet like a boxer in training.

Terri shook her head. 'Not exactly. I didn't know he was coming, but I'm glad he did.' Now why had she said that? Why had she given the impression that she enjoyed Kiel's company?

'If he's touched you——' began Barry, his lips tight, eyes as hard as bullets.

'He hasn't,' she cut in hurriedly, 'and I'm not standing here listening to you two arguing. I'm going to bed.' She hurried into her bedroom and then leaned back against the door, aware of the loud angry voices, understanding Barry's anger.

It seemed an age before the outer door finally closed and Kiel left. She expected Barry to come in to her, was surprised when he went through to his own room. She heard him moving about, and finally there was silence.

She appreciated him respecting her privacy, but would have liked to know what the conclusion had been. Was Barry still angry? Did he believe that nothing had been going on between them? Or had Kiel failed to convince him?

It would have been a simple matter to go and ask, but fearing the worst she felt reluctant, and dispiritedly climbed into bed instead. The best time to question Barry was in the morning when tempers had cooled.

But she could not help wondering what would have happened if Barry had not returned when he did. She had no idea what had prompted her to stop in front of Kiel. It had been tempting fate, and yet something had compelled her, an inner force stronger than her own mind.

CHAPTER FOUR

WHEN Terri awoke the next morning, it took her a few seconds to recall where she was. Looking out of the window she saw that the mountains, which had lost their shape during the hours of darkness, had become clear. And yet, even as she watched, a mist descended, obliterating, concealing.

Somewhere in the distance a train rattled its way across the countryside, a lamb bleated pitifully. Then gradually, as the sun grew stronger, the clouds lifted and the light was so clear she could see each granite outcrop on the mountains, each mound and hollow, each leaf on the nearby trees.

What a tapestry of colours! she thought in delight. How she wished she could stay longer. There was so much to see. Instead, once Kiel had found a replacement she would be on her way home.

What would Richard think, when she descended upon them? She wouldn't be able to stay with him and Rachel, of course. It wouldn't be fair. She would have to find a place of her own—and another job, which wouldn't be easy. But at least she wouldn't be stuck for money.

The house had been left to them jointly and she had taken her half in cash. It had seemed the best arrangement when Richard and Rachel decided to get married. He took out a mortgage for her half and she moved out. The house where she had been so happily brought up was no longer her home.

She had told herself it was about time she saw more of England than the city of London. Holidays had

59

always been spent abroad with her parents and she was ignorant about her homeland.

The Lakes were central to both England and Scotland and she had planned to explore extensively—until Kiel cruelly dashed her hopes. She could still hang on around here, she supposed, but the chances of a job were remote. In that respect at least she would be better off in London.

She sighed deeply and after washing and dressing went through to the kitchen and put on the kettle. There was no sign of Barry yet, she guessed it would be another hour before he put in an appearance.

After several cups of tea and a half packet of biscuits, which was all she could find for breakfast, Terri decided to take another walk and drink in more of this marvellous landscape. She had heard people enthuse over the Lakes, but always had been sceptical, believing nowhere could be that beautiful, not in England. But this was indeed a place apart—and she had seen only a tiny portion of it!

Yesterday she had chosen a little-used track, today she kept to the main road leading away from the town. She would explore Windermere another day. She wanted the wide open spaces, somewhere to breathe and forget all the traumas that were suddenly besetting her.

After her parents' tragic death she had been very emotional. They had a close-knit family, and to lose them both at the same time had seemed like the end of the world. But gradually her life had settled into its new routine and apart from her mistake getting involved with Greg she was happy enough.

Now Kiel was threatening that happiness. All sorts of unforeseen difficulties were rearing their ugly heads.

Suddenly she came upon a lake, small compared

with Windermere, and at this moment still and silent. The water looked silky-smooth and inviting and she wondered whether swimming was safe, or indeed if it was allowed.

All around rose majestic mountains. She supposed that somewhere were Scafell Pike and Skiddaw, which she knew were two of the highest and oldest mountains, but she had no idea of the names of the ones surrounding her.

As she stood in contemplation the silence was broken by the purr of a car's engine. She looked along the road and saw a white shape zooming swiftly towards her, but not until it drew closer did she realise it was Kiel.

Hastily she stepped back into the shelter of some trees, not wanting these quiet moments spoilt by the man who was doing his best to ruin her chances of contentment.

But she was too late. He stopped the car and walked down the gradual slope to stand by her side. 'You're up early. What's wrong, has my charming stepbrother kicked you out of his bed?'

Terri clamped her lips. Trust him to say something like that! 'As a matter of fact I haven't seen Barry since I left you two arguing last night.'

He threw her a doubtful glance. 'I find that very difficult to believe. Barry, in the same flat as a woman, and he doesn't touch her? It could never happen.'

'Then you think what you want to think,' snapped Terri. 'Do you always arrive at the surgery this early, or have you a call to make? I should hate to hold you up.'

His lips curled wryly. 'I'm going nowhere. Like you, I couldn't sleep.'

Terri looked out across the water, kicking her toes in the grey pebbles on its gently shelving banks. She was very aware of this man beside her, of the sexual magnetism he exuded. It was like a magnet pulling her towards him with a strength that was terrifying. She moved a few feet away, but he followed.

She turned blazing violet eyes in his direction. 'I wish you'd leave me in peace!' Peace! There would be no more of that today. He had ruined what promised to be a relaxing half hour.

'It's far too beautiful a morning to shut myself up any earlier than I have to,' he said pleasantly, ignoring her outburst. 'I have a boat tied up a little further along the shore. Nothing spectacular, I must admit—a plain and simple rowing boat. But if you've never been out on the Lakes in the early morning, before they're invaded by the holidaymakers who use this area as their playground, then you're in for a treat. Come with me, Teresa.'

It took her only a moment to reach a decision. It was an offer she could not resist. She was glad she had pulled on a pair of jeans and flat pumps and was soon scrambling eagerly over the bows of the boat, sitting facing him as he locked in the oars.

He pulled strongly and expertly, feathering the water with the blades on his return stroke. A motor would have spoilt this moment, would have ruined the heavenly silence. Terri had never known anything like it. It was an experience that would live in her memory for ever.

Her anger melted and she turned to Kiel eagerly. 'Have you always lived in the Lakes?'

He smiled at her enthusiasm and shook his head. 'I was born, would you believe, in Birmingham? I lived there until I went to Oxford, then when I began my medical training I spent a holiday in Kendal with a fellow student. I was so enamoured with the Lakes that I decided when I qualified it was where I wanted to work.'

'I can't say I blame you,' said Terri. 'It's heavenly. I can't believe it's real.'

'I couldn't agree more,' he returned. 'Like you, I'd lived in a world so built up with houses, offices, shops and factories that I couldn't believe the first time I came here that there was so much open space. There's over eight hundred square miles, did you know that? It's said to be some of the most amazing scenery in the world, and I agree. I've travelled quite a lot, but I've never seen anything that compares. I'm always glad to be home.'

Terri looked at Kiel in amazement. He had not struck her as the type to wax eloquent over nature.

'Don't be surprised,' he laughed, accurately reading her mind. 'There were other men before me who fell in love with it. Think of Wordsworth, Coleridge, Southey. They too felt the power. It reaches out invisible fingers and pulls you into its heart until there's no escape. I've never wanted to leave. I doubt I ever will.'

'It is lovely,' admitted Terri. 'This is my first glimpse of it, but it certainly won't be my last. I shall come again one day.'

'Feel free to pay me a visit if you ever do,' he said casually.

Terri felt an acute pang of misery. Come and see me whenever you're in the area, just like he would say to anyone else. She meant nothing to him; he had just confirmed that. His heart would never skip a beat at the sight of her. She willed her own to quell its erratic pounding, trailing her fingers through the chill waters, tilting back her head to look up at the clear blue sky.

Kiel stopped rowing and they sat still in the centre of the lake, the boat hardly moving. 'Come here,' he said quietly. 'Come and sit by me.'

He slid to one side of his seat and exactly as he had

known she would Terri stood up and gingerly stepped forward. She could not help herself. She wanted to make the most of these last few minutes spent together. Her eyes were fixed on his face as though she was hypnotised.

And this was her undoing. She did not spot the coil of rope, and when it slipped beneath her foot she yelled and lurched sideways. Clutching wildly at the air, she was aware of Kiel's outstretched arm, but too late. She gave a shriek and fell head first overboard.

The waters were icy. Terri was not a very good swimmer and felt a moment's panic as they closed over her head. She seemed to be going down for ever and ever, and gasped frantically for air when finally she surfaced.

But almost before she had time to blink the water out of her eyes she was hauled back into the boat by Kiel's powerful arms. His laughter was loud and long, annoying Terri, who saw nothing funny at all in the situation.

'How dare you laugh at me!' she cried, shaking the water from her hair. 'It was a stupid place to leave a piece of rope. You might have warned me. Oh, I'm freezing!'

'You should have seen your face!' he grinned. 'I wish I'd had a camera. I've never seen such a picture of surprise. Do you often taken an early morning dip?'

'I might have drowned!' she thrust savagely.

He chuckled. 'I wouldn't have let you, but we'd best get you back to the car.'

By the time they reached the shore Terri could not keep a limb still, and dared not think what sort of a sight she looked. Kiel wrapped her in his car rug, cocooning her like a chrysalis, lifting her on to the seat because he had wrapped it so tightly she could not move. In the end she was laughing too. It was the only way, otherwise she would have cried.

The smile remained on his face throughout the short drive back to the surgery. Once there he swung her effortlessly into his arms and carried her up the steps to the flat.

Despite her shivers and the discomfort of being soaking wet, Terri felt an immediate response to the rock-hard body against which she was held. Breathing became difficult and she felt on fire, her heart banging along at twice its normal pace.

There was no disputing Kiel's sensual magnetism. but it was crazy feeling attracted at a time like this, especially when he had treated her so indifferently. He really could not care less what happened to her.

Barry frowned harshly when they entered, but Kiel gave him no more than a glance before kicking open Terri's bedroom door and depositing her inside. With one last laugh he said, 'There, I'll leave you to it.'

She heard the voices of the two men, but made no attempt to listen. Instead she struggled out of her wet clothes, wrapping a towel about her before going next door to the bathroom and standing beneath the stinging jets of hot water.

Uppermost in her mind was the feel of Kiel's body against hers and she found it impossible to banish him from her mind. But when she finally emerged, dressed in a clean blouse and skirt, her hair dry and neatly brushed, he had gone.

Disappointment welled, but she had no time to dwell on it. Barry banged a mug of tea down in front of her. 'What a damn fool you've made of yourself!'

Terri's fine brows rose questioningly. 'I couldn't help it. I didn't mean to fall in.'

'You shouldn't have been out there.'

She felt irritated by his unreasonable manner. 'I was

up early, I felt like a walk. How was I to know Kiel would come along?'

Barry pulled a wry face and sighed. 'I suppose you're right, but I hate the thought of you and him—being together.'

'Heavens,' cried Terri, 'he was being polite, that's all. Kiel will be glad to see the back of me.'

'And all because of me,' he said ruefully. 'I almost wish I'd never mentioned this job to Richard. I feel it's all my fault that things haven't turned out as you hoped.'

Terri shook her head. 'Don't say that. I'm glad I came. I'm glad I've seen all this. It's whetted my appetite and I shall definitely come back for a holiday.' She sipped her tea. 'About last night, did you really take Laura out after you'd seen to her mother?'

He looked guilty. 'I thought you'd be in bed and wouldn't need me.'

'It was in very bad taste,' Terri returned sharply, 'considering her mother was ill. And didn't it occur to you that I might be nervous on my own?'

He lowered his lids, his lips twisted, looking for all the world like a naughty schoolboy. 'I'm sorry, I won't do it again.'

Terri could not help laughing. She had seen Barry play the innocent so many times—and it always got him his own way.

Kiel was waiting in the surgery when she eventually went down, but this was Kiel the doctor, not the man. He was brisk and professional, informing and advising and then leaving her to it as the patients began to trickle in.

The morning went smoothly and quickly. Terri was surprised how busy they were. Afterwards Kiel and Barry went out on their rounds and she was left to fill in various records and generally tidy up.

Then, bearing in mind Kiel's instructions to get her tyre fixed, she switched the phone through to his housekeeper and drove in the direction of Windermere.

She found a garage on the outskirts of the town and while waiting for the repair browsed through the gift shops, mingling with the dozens of walkers in their strong boots and woolly socks, their short shorts and open-necked shirts. It made her realise exactly what she would miss when she left.

At evening surgery, Terry was again kept busy with dressings and various tests, as well as answering the telephone and making sure the incoming patients were directed to the doctors' consulting rooms in their correct order. Really, she thought, they could do with a receptionist as well as a nurse. There was far too much work for one person.

When eventually she went back up to the flat she said to Barry, 'I'm exhausted. All I want is a shower and bed.'

'At this hour?' he laughed. 'You must be mad!'

'I did have a long tiring day yesterday,' she said. 'I think it's catching up on me.'

He grinned. 'Actually I guessed you'd be too tired to go out, so I did some shopping. I'm no cook, though. You'll have to do it.'

Terri groaned. She didn't have the strength to stand over a stove. On the other hand, she was hungry. She's eaten nothing all day except a few biscuits, and a sandwich in Windermere. She stared in distaste at the potatoes waiting to be peeled. 'We'll go out.'

They did not linger long over their meal, Barry driving her straight back to the flat once they had eaten, so she could have her early night. She was surprised to see Kiel's car outside the surgery, but even more astonished to discover him in their flat.

The moment they entered he said, 'I have a patient to see, Teresa. I want you to come with me.'

Before she had time to speak Barry said heatedly, 'Why? You've never taken a nurse with you before. Besides, she's tired. She had a long drive yesterday, in case you've forgotten, and we have been extra busy—it's always the same on a Monday, as you well know. She wants to go to bed.'

But Terri had suddenly been injected with a new lease of life. 'I don't mind,' she said at once.

'Good!' Kiel hardly glanced at his stepbrother, except to say as they reached the door, 'Don't wait up, I'll see she gets in safely.'

'I bet you will!' snarled Barry, unable to hide his ill-humour, and Terri felt sure his annoyance went deeper than simply objecting to her working. He was jealous! He really was beginning to look upon her as something more than a platonic friend—despite Laura!

The thought was disquieting and she turned to Kiel as she settled herself in his car. 'I hope you haven't been waiting long?'

'I'd just arrived, and contrary to what Barry thinks I do appreciate how tired you must be. You've done well today.'

Praise indeed! 'I simply did my job,' she said modestly. 'Is it true that you don't normally take your nurse with you?'

He shrugged. 'I thought you'd enjoy the ride. I guess he didn't take too kindly to me whisking you away. Have I spoilt a promising evening?' There was a sudden tightening to his jaw and the glance he gave her had lost its friendliness.

She lifted her brows and her violet eyes shot sparks across the space dividing them. 'I was going to bed—alone! And if the reason you've got me out here is to give me another lecture on the inadvisability of having an affair with Barry, then you're wasting your breath.'

'Because whatever I say will make no difference?' His steely glance cut through her like a knife.

'There's no difference for it to make,' she tossed. 'Barry means nothing to me, not in the way you're thinking.'

'Do you know——' the smile was back '—I think I'm beginning to believe you.'

Terri cast him a doubting glance. 'I'm glad, because that's the way it is.'

'But not the way Barry would like it, eh? That's why he encouraged you to come here?'

Terri was growing tired of his continuous insinuations. 'I've given up arguing.'

'Are you denying, then, that he has any interest in you?'

'Yes, I am,' she said strongly, wishing she felt as confident as she sounded. Barry's attitude towards her had definitely changed.

'It's not how it looks to me,' said Kiel. 'He's one hell of a protective guy where you're concerned. He told me in no uncertain terms to keep my hands off you, and that must surely mean he's interested himself?'

'It means he's concerned about me—as a friend,' insisted Terri, wondering when he was going to give up. She could not see where any of this was leading.

Kiel shook his head, smiling to himself. 'I've never known Barry have a spiritual relationship with a woman.'

Terri lifted her shoulders. 'There's no more to be said then, is there?' She turned her head determinedly away and silence settled between them.

Even so Terri could not ignore him. She was aware of every movement he made, of his attraction for her.

She had felt it the very first time they met and none of what had happened made any difference.

There was something about him that set him apart from other men, and even though all she was doing was filling a gap until he could find another nurse, she could not dismiss those feelings.

She tried to concentrate on the passing scenery. They were driving along a narrow winding lane with drystone walls on either side. They passed through sleepy little hamlets with grey cottages, over hump-backed bridges revealing sudden vistas of different-coloured fields criss-crossed with yet more stone walls. Ox-eye daisies and pink bladder-campion grew along the roadside, brilliant yellow St John's wort and pale blue harebells. A butterfly's paradise.

Kiel drove fast and confidently, knowing every inch of the road, and inevitably Terri's gaze came back to him, to the capable hands on the wheel, the long legs stretched out in front, the fine material of his trousers pulled taut across muscular thighs.

'This is Dockray,' he said, suddenly breaking the silence. 'Where they hold the Shepherd's Meet.'

'Where shepherds meet?' smiled Terri, glad the tension had been broken. She did not think she could have stood it another mile.

She had been jesting and was surprised when he laughed and said, 'Right in one. Every other year the farmers meet here and hand over any stray sheep that have turned up on their land. After the official handing-over ceremony they celebrate at the Royal Hotel, talking shop, drinking each other's health, and singing Lakeland songs. It's a good excuse for letting down their hair.'

'Sounds fun,' said Terri, 'but why not every year?'

'Because,' he informed her, 'on the years in between they celebrate at the King's Head in Thirlspot, an historic inn that was frequently patronised by William Wordsworth and Dorothy, his sister.'

'I see,' nodded Terri, then eagerly, 'Talking of Wordsworth, I'd really like to see Dove Cottage before I go home.'

'I'll take you,' he offered surprisingly. 'I know I oughtn't to admit this, but I've never been there myself. We'll look at the place together.'

Terri tried her hardest not to show her pleasure. Things were looking good all of a sudden. Kiel seemed to have forgotten his animosity—though for how long was anybody's guess. His swift mood changes were something she would never get used to.

The road began to climb suddenly and they branched off along a valley between two immense fells, their long sweeping slopes seeming to stretch for ever skywards.

Then without warning he stopped the car in front of a farmhouse. Terri followed as he strode indoors, seeing yet another side of Kiel as he spoke softly and reassuringly to the elderly farmer who had been badly bitten by a stray dog he had caught worrying his sheep.

When Kiel was working his whole attitude was so different it was difficult to believe he was the same man. He was gentle and caring, establishing a confidence and rapport with his patient, which counted for far more than the actual medical side. Terri could see now why he was so popular, why so many people came to him when they could easily have attended elsewhere.

The farmer's wife had a cup of tea waiting and they spent a further pleasant half hour putting the world to rights, before Kiel suggested they leave.

Darkness had fallen and there was nothing to be seen on the drive home apart from the grey winding road picked out in the tunnel of Kiel's headlamps. Terri sank her head back on her seat and closed her eyes, comforted by the thought of Kiel beside her.

She knew nothing more until she heard him say, 'Wake up, we're back.' To her alarm she discovered her head on his shoulder. He had stopped the car and his arm was protectively about her.

Sleepily she looked up into his face, glad of the darkness to hide her embarrassment. 'I'm sorry, it was rude of me to go to sleep.' But exceedingly exciting to be held in the crook of his arm. She would have liked to remain a while longer.

'Don't apologise, I know you're tired. But your self-appointed guardian is waiting.' His voice hardened on these last words.

An outside light was switched on and Barry came bouncing down the steps, wrestling open the car door, taking in at a glance Kiel's arm about her.

Terri dragged herself free and with a sleepy, 'Good night, Kiel,' stumbled up the stairs to the flat.

'You've been a long time,' accused Barry as he closed the door behind them. 'What have you been doing?'

Terri looked at him from beneath heavy lids. 'Helping Kiel. For goodness' sake, Barry, don't give me the third degree now, I'm too tired. I'm going to bed.'

'Don't you even want a drink?'

She shook her head and closed her bedroom door and, almost before her head settled on the pillow, was asleep.

The next morning Terri woke early, feeling completely refreshed and glad to be alive. And all because of the closeness she had felt to Kiel last night.

She showered and pulled on a clean dress, smiling to herself when she saw the supply of eggs on the table. She heard Barry getting up, so she toasted some bread and scrambled eggs, and breakfast was ready when he came through.

'I didn't expect you up yet,' he said.

She stretched her arms above her head and grinned. 'I slept like a log and now I'm fighting fit. I know I shouldn't say this, but I really am enjoying working here. I shall be sorry to go.'

'Are you sure it's the work,' he asked sharply, 'and not my beguiling stepbrother? He appears to have got over his antagonism. Are you sure you're not losing your head over him? It wouldn't be wise, you know. I should hate you to get hurt. He won't change his mind about keeping you on.'

Terri laughed, she couldn't help it—a high lilting melodious sound that filled the room.

Barry looked hurt. 'What's so funny?'

'You and Kiel,' she giggled, 'you're both warning me against the other. It's too ridiculous for words!'

'I don't call being taken in by Kiel ridiculous,' he said gruffly.

'I know exactly what he's like,' she said. 'He has no interest in me, although I must confess I do find him attractive. I've no intention of letting myself fall in love with him, though.' Or at least she wasn't admitting this to Barry. 'I shall be gone from here soon, there's no point.' Except that she was already more than halfway there. It was something she could not help, it was stealing over her as surely as night follows day.

'I'm glad you're being sensible,' he said, 'but do be careful. He can be a dangerous man to tangle with. I don't want you eating your heart out over some guy who's not worthy of you.'

She smiled. He was being over-protective. 'I appreciate your concern.' She hoped it was no more than that, she really hoped Barry wasn't seeing her in that light himself.

'Richard will expect me to look after you. What do you think he'll say if you go home with a broken heart because you've fallen for that handsome stepbrother of mine? Now if it was me it would be a different matter.'

Terri ignored the meaningful look he gave her. 'If it did happen there'd be nothing Richard could do about it, but it won't. I'm not falling in love for a long time.' She bit into her toast and crunched on it determinedly.

But throughout the day when contact with Kiel was inevitable she realised just how deeply her feelings ran. It was fortunate he treated her with clinical detachment, not seeing her as a person, more like a robot who automatically did whatever she was told.

The work was interesting but arduous and by the end of the week she was exhausted. 'You look like a shadow,' said Barry. 'Come on, I'm taking you out. Kiel has no right pushing you so hard.'

'I don't mind,' protested Terri. 'In fact I'm enjoying it.' But it was punishing work and too much for one person. Even when the doctors were out there was still paperwork to be done and the phone never seemed to stop ringing.

The hotel Barry took her to was tucked away at the foot of a mountain, an olde-worlde restaurant with alcoves and velvet-covered seats, the food superb. Terri ate ravenously until she felt ready to burst.

'There's a tiny lake not far from here,' Barry said when they had finished. 'It's well off the beaten track and usually there's no one about. How about a stroll?'

Terri nodded. 'I need it after that. I'll never sleep on such a full stomach.'

He parked the car as near as possible to the lake and they walked through a wood, the slender branches topped with an umbrella of delicate green foliage. There was bracken underfoot and soft springy turf. Terri's high-heeled sandals were not exactly ideal for walking and Barry held her hand, helping her in the difficult places.

There was none of the awareness she felt with Kiel. With Barry she felt nothing.

They paused and he skimmed pebbles across the surface of the lake. The water lapped gently on the shore. It was the only sound, even the birds were silent.

Barry suddenly stopped what he was doing and looked at her. 'You're very beautiful, Terri, do you know that? You're a very . . . desirable woman.'

Her heart stopped as she remembered the way he had treated her on her sixteenth birthday. She hoped he wasn't going to start that all over again. Perhaps it hadn't been very wise to come out here with him tonight?

'I've had to struggle to resist you these last few days,' he went on. 'How do you feel, Terri—about me? Do you think . . .?'

'Please, Barry,' she stopped him quickly, 'don't talk that way. You'll always be like a brother to me, nothing more. I like you, I like you a lot, but not in the manner you're suggesting.' She felt the whole thing distasteful.

'Let's go back,' he said suddenly, harshly, and without waiting began to retrace his steps.

Terri was glad, but for the first time there was an uneasy atmosphere between them. She wished he hadn't voiced his feelings. What she had only suspected she could ignore. Now, knowing how he felt, it would be impossible sleeping in the same flat.

As soon as they got indoors he poured himself a large whisky and downed it in one swallow. Terri felt alarmed because he had already drunk half a bottle of wine. She wanted to go to bed, but was afraid that if she left him he would drink the whole bottle. He was in a very strange mood.

So she accepted a glass of whisky herself, topping it with water and sipping slowly. Barry drank his neat, but after his third she said, 'I don't think you ought to drink any more.'

'It's the only way I'll get any sleep tonight,' he said thickly. Then abruptly he growled, 'Dammit!' and lurched towards her. Before she could stop him he pulled her into his arms and showered her face with hot feverish kisses.

Terri recoiled. This was a side to Barry that she didn't like at all. But his arms imprisoned her and his hot lips sought hers eagerly. 'God, I want you,' he muttered. 'Why don't you relax and enjoy it? You're a full-blooded woman now, not a kid of sixteen. Kiss me, Terri. Kiss me!'

Nausea rose in her throat and she struggled desperately to free herself, but he clung like a man demented, assaulting her body with an insolence she found degrading.

'Let me go!' she cried, when his thigh thrust between her legs. 'Let me go this instant. How dare you do this to me?'

'Kiel's not going to be the only one to make love to you,' he slurred. 'Why should he always be lucky? You're mine, Terri, not his.' He swung her into his arms and carried her struggling through to his bedroom, throwing her down on the bed and himself on top.

His eager hands tore at the neck of her dress and Terri fought with every atom of strength, clawing, kicking, biting, but her attempts were futile. Whisky had given him added strength, had made him like an animal She was afraid, desperately afraid.

She finally acknowledged that Kiel did indeed know Barry better than she. She had not known he could behave in this manner. She had expected him to take no for an answer. What a fool she had been!

But he had wanted her before touching the whisky! Drink had merely added fuel to his fire. She had to get out before he went any further.

CHAPTER FIVE

IT was no use screaming because there was no one to hear, and fighting would only make him more determined. Perhaps appealing to his better nature might help?

'Barry,' she pleaded, her voice low and tremulous, 'you're going to hate yourself in the morning. Why don't you stop now before it's too late and everything's ruined between us?'

She relaxed beneath him and momentarily he too ceased his frenzied movements, 'Are you trying to say you don't want me?' His face leered over her. 'Enjoy yourself, no one's going to disturb us.'

That was what she was afraid of.

'I could kick myself when I realise how much time I've wasted. We could have had so much fun.'

Terri squirmed beneath him, renewing her struggles. 'I don't want you to kiss me, Barry. I don't want you to even touch me.'

'Why not?' he mouthed thickly, his words slurring into each other. 'You don't object to Kiel touching you. Why should he be the lucky one when he's done you no good turns? He can have any woman he wants, Terri.'

'And so can you,' she cried. 'You don't have to force yourself on me. Barry, please, you're spoiling our friendship!'

'Spoil?' he snarled. 'How can making love to a beautiful woman spoil anything? It's what women are for. Come on, Terri, kiss me. Let me show you what you've been missing.'

'No, Barry, *no!*' She rolled her head away from his demanding mouth, but he caught her face between his hands, pinning it down, forcing her lips apart, plundering her with his eager tongue.

Terri felt sick and clamped her teeth. He yelled and shot backwards.

'Why, you . . .' he began, then the next second she was miraculously free. She caught a glimpse of Kiel's livid face as he dragged Barry off her.

Almost immediately there was the sickening sound of fist meeting jaw and by the time she struggled up Barry was lying on the floor.

'My God, what have you done?' she asked when he did not move.

Kiel glared at Terri savagely. 'I've given him no more than he deserves. But I blame you for encouraging him.' He spat out the words between gritted teeth, his face taut and white with an anger that shook his whole frame. 'To think I was beginning to believe you when you said he was no more than a friend. Some friend!'

Terri stared aghast. 'He forced me. Surely you don't think that——'

'I prefer to believe my own eyes,' he cut in harshly. 'Looks like some party you had.' He eyed the glasses and almost empty bottle of whisky. 'I should have known he'd go back to it. Encourage him, did you?'

'I don't know what you mean.' Terri frowned and glanced from Kiel to the bottle and back again to the grim-faced man who was filling the room with his presence. He was so powerful he was threatening to choke her, and she swallowed several times as she waited for his explanation.

'Don't tell me you had no idea Barry had a drink problem?' The potent silver glitter of his eyes never left her face, but before she could speak, he continued,

'Since he qualified he's left it strictly alone—he's had
to, otherwise he knows what would happen. And his
father certainly wouldn't be pleased if he was struck
off. But I should have known it was too good to be
true.' This last was delivered with a sneer that brought
an ugly curl to his lips.

Terri backed a pace, feeling almost as if she had
been struck. 'Do you mean he is—he was—an
alcoholic?'

'As good as,' grated Kiel. 'Are you trying to tell me
you didn't know? My God, what an innocent you are!
It appears you don't know Barry at all.'

She shook her head in bewilderment. 'I didn't. I
really never knew him.'

'But now you do,' he rasped, 'and you're not staying
here a moment longer. Get your things together,
you're coming home with me.'

'To your house?' It would be like leaping out of the
proverbial frying pan into the fire.

'Where else?' he demanded. 'Don't worry, you'll
be safe. Get going.' He gave her a push as Barry
finally hauled himself to his feet and took a lunge at
him.

Terri went through to her room as if in a dream,
aghast when she caught sight of her reflection. She
looked like a wild woman, hair tangled, skin white
beneath blotchy make-up, lips bruised and swollen,
her dress torn.

She ripped it off in distaste and would have loved to
take a shower but was afraid to keep Kiel waiting.
There was an ominous silence in the room outside,
and her fingers trembled as she stuffed clothes into her
case.

At last she was ready. She opened the door and the
two men stood poised like tigers, each waiting for the
other to make the first move.

Barry's jaw was cut and bleeding and there were scratches down his cheek where she had clawed him in her frenzy. He really did look a sight. His eyelids were heavy and he swayed on his feet. She did not like leaving him in this state, but her fear of him was much stronger, and she gladly accompanied Kiel outside.

Neither spoke on the journey. Terri was beginning to get used to these silences, and tonight of all times there was nothing to say. Every limb trembled and she could not rid from her mind Barry's unprecedented attack.

She had never dreamed he would treat her like this. She had felt quite safe sharing his flat, despite Kiel's innuendoes. A tremor ran through her as she recalled how he had forced his kisses on her, nausea rose in her throat, and she knew she would never forget that moment.

They arrived at Kiel's house and made their way inside. Almost immediately a small, slim, middle-aged woman appeared, giving Terri a curious look.

'Ah, Mrs Barnes,' said Kiel. 'Would you kindly get a room ready for Miss Denning. She'll be staying for—er—a short while.'

When she had disappeared Kiel said, 'Now, what would you like? A hot drink? Something stronger?'

She shook her head violently. 'Not whisky. I'll never drink whisky again without remembering today.' A shudder ran through her. 'It was horrible!'

Kiel led her into the small sitting-room they had used before. 'It was on the cards. You're very attractive.'

'But there was no need for him to behave like an animal!'

'What was wrong, wasn't he getting his own way?'

She shook her head violently. 'Nor will he ever!'

His brows rose at the vehemence in her tone. 'Sit

down, I'll organise a mug of hot chocolate. That should settle you for the night.'

She doubted it. She doubted whether she would settle at all, not after what had happened. Her skin crawled every time she thought about Barry's hands pawing her body. It was the most frightening thing that had ever happened to her.

Kiel was gone for no more than a couple of minutes. 'Mrs Barnes will be along with our drinks just as soon as she's made up your bed.' He sat beside her on the couch, his eyes gentle as they rested on her face.

'I'm being a nuisance, aren't I?' Terri's own eyes were wide and troubled.

He shook his head. 'I wouldn't have brought you here if I hadn't wanted to. I'd have booked you into a hotel.'

She was still not convinced. 'I suppose you're saying that because you know I won't be here long. I know how jealously you guard your privacy.'

He frowned and took her hand, but she snatched away.

'Hey,' he said softly, 'I'm not Barry.'

'I can't help it.' Her voice was pained. 'I don't want anyone to touch me. I feel unclean. I'd like a bath.'

He looked angry with himself all of a sudden. 'I should have thought of that. Damn Barry! I wish I'd done a better job on him. I'll get Mrs B. to run you one after she's made our drinks, and then you can go straight to bed.'

'I can do it myself,' Terri demurred, not used to such treatment.

'Nonsense,' he smiled. 'Mrs B. won't mind. She's always complaining she hasn't enough to do.'

At that moment the woman entered carrying a tray loaded with two steaming mugs and a plate of home-made biscuits. 'I've put Miss Denning in the yellow room,' she said. 'It's ready as soon as she is.'

'Which won't be long,' said Kiel, 'but she'd like a bath first. Would you mind? And then you can go to bed. Teresa's very concerned that she's putting you to a lot of trouble.'

The woman smiled. 'Not at all. It's a pleasure to have someone to look after.' Again that curious look. 'It's rare we have guests.' She hustled out, and Terri could actually believe she enjoyed the extra work.

Cupping the mug between her hands, Terri sipped her drink. Gradually the warmth seeped back into her bruised bones and she was aware of Kiel watching her with concern in his eyes.

But she was glad he made no further attempt to touch her. She did not feel she would like any man ever to touch her again. She couldn't believe Barry had behaved so badly. He had spoilt the lovely relationship they had had for so long. She would never be able to look him in the eye again. And what was she going to tell Richard? How could she explain that his best friend had attacked her like that?

She shook her head, her eyes filling with tears, and Kiel, astutely guessing her thoughts, said, 'It will fade, like all bad things.'

'It was so awful, so degrading,' she whispered, tears rolling down her cheeks. It was unusual for her to cry, in fact she could not remember doing so since her parents died. She had had to be strong since then, but now she felt as though all the strength had drained from her.

He passed her a handkerchief and she dabbed her eyes. He looked as though he would have liked to pull her into his arms, but respecting her wishes waited patiently until she had calmed herself.

'Drink up now,' he said. 'You look all in. I suppose

in a way it's my fault. We've been unusually busy this
last week, but you've coped admirably, and if it wasn't
for Barry I'd seriously consider keeping you on. I
can't get rid of him, though, much as I'd like to.' A
fierce scowl creased his brow. 'If he wasn't family I
would, but I can't hurt our respective parents.' His
voice grew stronger. 'Hell, Teresa, if he lays another
finger on you I'll kill him!'

She was shocked by the venom in his tone and
couldn't think why he should feel so protective when
he had previously accused her of being as bad as
Barry. He surely hadn't had a change of heart?

The moment she finished her drink he said,
'Upstairs with you. I'll put your case in your room
and Mrs B. can lay out your nightclothes.'

They mounted the stairs together. Terri ached from
head to toe and thought she would never make it.
Even so, she could not bear the thought of Kiel
helping her. It would take time to forget what Barry
had done.

She managed a smile when she discovered that her
bedroom was as far away from Kiel's as it could
possibly be. Good old Mrs Barnes, she thought.
Thank heaven she observed proprieties!

She almost fell asleep in the bath and was brought
back to the present when the housekeeper knocked and
asked whether she needed any help. Even then she was
so long in answering that the woman came into the
room.

'Dr Braden was worried about you,' she said,
picking up a towel and holding it out.

Terri took the towel and cocooned herself in it.
'Thank you, Mrs Barnes, I'll be all right now.'

But the woman still lingered. 'I don't like leaving
you. Dr Braden said I was to make sure you were
safely in bed.'

'Safe?' Terri's tone was high. 'What does he think's going to happen to me here?' But his thoughtfulness warmed her and as she towelled herself dry and shrugged into the nightdress Mrs Barnes had unpacked, her thoughts were more on him than his obnoxious stepbrother.

She climbed between the sheets and Mrs Barnes tucked her in as her mother used to do. It was oddly comforting. She felt like a child again.

But even though she was warm, Terri could not relax and found it difficult to sleep. Each time she closed her eyes she saw Barry's flushed menacing face. Lust, that's what it had been. He had wanted her for her body alone. She shuddered.

Eventually she fell asleep, only to be disturbed by violent dreams of numerous faceless men assaulting her, and she woke in a panic, her body drenched with perspiration.

She showered and dressed and then discovered it was only six. So she sat at the long windows that came right down to the floor, admiring the panoramic view she had previously only seen at night.

It was as magnificent as she expected. The tiny lake far below shone like a mirror. She was not sure whether it was the same one she had fallen into. She thought it might be, unwittingly came back memories of being carried in Kiel's arms, of the feeling of strength and power that were an integral part of him. She felt safe here in his house.

Although they were high there were still peaks towering above them, some areas tree-clad, others wild and barren. The nearest hills were clearly defined, but as her eyes moved further away the scenery became indistinct until finally the hills were nothing more than a purple haze.

How long she sat there she was not sure, but she

was brought out of her reverie by a tap on the door.
'Come in,' she called, expecting Mrs Barnes, then was
surprised when Kiel himself entered.

He too was freshly showered, looking as handsome
as Barry had said, in a pair of brown cords and a silk
knit beige shirt. He smiled warmly. 'How are you? I
heard you moving about. Why are you up so early?'

'I kept having nightmares,' admitted Terri, ap-
preciating his concern and glad of his company.

He nodded understandingly. 'It was a traumatic
experience. I blame myself for having thrust you
together.'

She shook her head. 'You weren't to know. Besides,
I felt quite safe. I thought I knew Barry. I didn't know
he could be like that.'

'Well, I did,' he said strongly. 'The truth of the
matter is I really thought you and he were lovers, or
wanted to be. Thank goodness I came round last
night.'

'Why did you?' she asked.

'I called in at the surgery to pick up some supplies
and heard the commotion.' He moved across the room
and stood by her chair. The musky scent of his
aftershave filled Terri's nostrils and she felt a sudden
longing to be held against that firm, hard body. There
would be comfort in his arms. He was the one man she
would never be afraid of.

He had once said he never kissed a woman unless
she was willing, and she believed him. She could see
why he despised his stepbrother so much and
wondered how Barry could have kept this side of him
hidden from her and Richard all these years.

Perhaps it was because they saw him so infrequently
these days? It could have developed recently. He
probably drank to boost his morale; to put him, in his
own mind, on equal terms with Kiel.

It must be difficult for Barry to be constantly compared with this older, successful man. She could understand why he resented him. Barry probably wished his father had never remarried. Perhaps that was when it all started? Barry had never discussed Kiel and now she thought she could understand why.

'If you're up to it I thought we'd go to Dove Cottage?' His eyes were surprisingly gentle, his voice soft.

'But what about the surgery?'

'Saturday's always quiet. Barry can cope. Besides, I owe myself a day off, and you could do with a break.'

Terri smiled. 'I certainly could! There's more work than I expected—not that I'm complaining,' she added quickly. 'I like it.'

He nodded. 'Good. We'll take a leisurely breakfast and then go. Are you sure you're all right? No after-effects?'

Terri appreciated his concern. 'None at all.'

'Come, then,' he said, 'we'll tell Mrs B. and take a stroll in the garden while she cooks breakfast.'

The garden blended perfectly with their sur-roundings. It was difficult to see where the long sloping lawns ended and the countryside proper began.

There were shrubberies and rose beds and the long uncluttered lines were pleasing to the eye. They were able to walk right round the house and get a different view from each side.

'This must be the most peaceful place on earth,' said Terri as they sat on a bench strategically placed to get the best view.

Kiel shrugged. 'It's pretty grim in winter. If the snow's bad, I stay at the flat. Some of the roads become impassable and yet, ironically, it's when we're most busy.'

And she wouldn't be a part of it! A fleeting sadness washed over Terri. But in a way it was best she was going. Working with Barry would be impossible now.

Almost as though he could read her thoughts, Kiel said, 'If you weren't attracted to Barry why did you decide to come and work here?'

Terri shrugged. 'Because I wanted a change from London. I had to get out of the house anyway because my brother's just got married and he doesn't want me living with him. I've sold him my half and I suppose when I go back I'll find myself a flat or something.'

He frowned. 'But he will let you live with him until you find somewhere, won't he? I didn't realise you were—homeless.'

Terri glanced at him from beneath lowered lids. Would it have made any difference if he had known? She doubted it. He would still have insisted she leave. 'He won't throw me out in the street.'

'Have you told him yet that you're returning?'

'No!'

He glanced at her sharply. 'Why's that? Did you think I might change my mind?' His tone was suddenly suspicious.

'Not in the least,' said Terri quickly. 'I simply didn't want to worry him, not while he's still in the first blissful throes of marriage. He's looked after me since my parents died. It's about time I stood on my own feet.'

'Does he know you've been sharing Barry's flat?'

Terri shook her head, her lips tightening, a shadow crossing her face. 'I can't get over the way he changed last night. One moment he was the Barry I knew, the next he had become a monster.'

Kiel's eyes darkened with anger. 'To be quite honest I think it was his way of hurting me. He feels that we—you and I—are getting too friendly. He doesn't realise that when people work together there's no point in showing hostilities. To put it bluntly, he's jealous.'

'Surely not?' frowned Terri. 'There's nothing to be jealous about.' She tried to ignore the swift stab of pain his brusque words caused. He could not have made his feelings any clearer had he tried.

'Barry can't keep any girl for long, whereas I never have the same problem. It's as simple as that. And I'm sure it's why he made those demands on you last night.'

'I see,' said Terri. Barry had an inferiority complex which he would never get rid of while working with Kiel. She wondered why their respective parents couldn't see it. Thrusting them together was making things worse. It wasn't helping Barry. He needed to make something of his life without Kiel breathing over his shoulder. He ought not to be working in the same practice at all.

'Let's not talk about Barry any longer,' he said briskly. 'I don't want him to spoil our day. Let's go and see if breakfast's ready.'

Terri's breakfast never usually consisted of anything more than a couple of slices of toast and when she saw the laden table she was taken aback. Cereals, covered dishes, a rack of toast, pots of honey, jam and marmalade. Home-made crusty rolls. It was all there.

To her surprise she managed a little of everything, but nothing like the amount Kiel consumed. He had a voracious appetite, she discovered.

And then they were ready to go. It was not a very long drive and Terri was too busy looking about her to want to talk.

Grasmere was a pretty little village with lots of souvenir and gift shops, artists' studios and a garden centre, but they did not linger long, nor did they look at Wordsworth's grave in the churchyard.

Instead they walked on to Dove Cottage where the poet had lived with his sister and, later, his wife. It was a small white building with a grey-tiled roof and a wall in front.

Inside it was preserved as it had been in Wordsworth's day and Terri could imagine them living here, the flames leaping from the black-leaded grate in the kitchen, the occupants sleeping in the iron beds.

Nearby a barn had been converted into a museum which housed his major manuscripts, first editions, and some of his personal belongings. It was all Terri could do to drag herself away. She was fascinated.

'Now what?' asked Kiel, when eventually they emerged back out into the bright sunlight.

Terri shrugged. 'Anything you show me will be new.'

He thought for a moment. 'How about Langdale Pikes and then over the passes? It's an experience you ought not to miss.'

'If you say so,' she smiled, quite content to leave the decisions to him.

'That's Loughrigg Fell on your left,' he informed her as they set off. 'It's quite easy to climb and the views of Lakeland are superb. Do you fancy it?'

Terri shook her head. 'I'm not dressed for climbing.' Which was a pity, because she would have liked to go up there with Kiel.

He pointed out a tarn. 'It's an ice-skater's paradise in winter.' And Elterwater. 'Not large enough to be called a lake, but not small enough for a tarn.' He was a mine of information.

Then suddenly Great Langdale lay ahead and the Pikes rose so sharply above them that Terri felt they were being walled in. They dominated the whole landscape.

'What does pike mean?' she asked. She had no fear he would not know the answer. He knew everything about the Lakes.

'It comes from the Norse word *pik*,' he said, 'meaning a sharp point—a peak. As a matter of fact most of the names around here have Norse origins. About a thousand years ago Norsemen from Ireland and the Isle of Man settled here. Even the streams are called becks from the Norse word *bekkr*, the waterfalls are forces, from the word *foss*, and the mountain lakes are tarns from the Norse, *tjorn*.'

The pikes were barbarous and uncompromising, yet despite this incredibly beautiful. Terri could see why they attracted so many climbers. They were dotted now with people scaling the sometimes sheer walls.

A couple of miles further on the road curved and they arrived at the two Dungeon Ghyll hotels. They had lunch at one of them and then Kiel took her to Dungeon Ghyll Force. The walk from the hotel took them about twenty minutes, the path climbing steeply, and when they got there Terri could see from where the waterfall got its name.

It was not very high but the rocky walls through which the water cascaded were like those of some huge grim prison cell. She listened to the water rushing and falling, splashing and dripping, admired the droplets sparkling on ferns like morning dew. It was a place of sheer beauty and she said impulsively, 'I'm so glad you brought me here. I shall never forget it.'

He looked pleased. 'I thought you might like it. You and I have similar tastes. But there are other more spectacular falls than this one, although they're all beautiful in their own right.'

His words warmed Terri and she felt the rapport

grow between them. He drove through to Little Langdale where the air in the valley was noticeably warmer, and a little further on they came to a junction. Here they headed towards Wrynose Pass.

'According to local history,' he told her, 'this area was popular with smugglers in the seventeenth century. They brought their liquor here from the coast, along the pass, and stored it in the cellars of farmhouses near Little Langdale Tarn.'

'I always associate smugglers with Cornwall,' said Terri.

'Smuggling went on in the most surprising places,' he told her. 'But when it was no longer practicable, some of the locals distilled their own whisky. One of the most famous characters was Lanty Slee who produced his "hell brew" in Bessy Crag quarry above the tarn.'

Suddenly Terri found herself pressed back in her seat. The road rose sharply with fierce bends at impossibly steep angles. It was so narrow that the only way two cars could pass was in the specially provided passing places. Terri was horrified.

But when she looked at Kiel he was smiling. 'Are you enjoying it?'

'Enjoying it?' she cried. 'I'm terrified! I never realised there were roads like this.'

'Lakeland is a mixture of everything,' he grinned.

Sometimes the road dropped away completely and Terri clung to the edge of her seat, imagining them falling over the edge. At the summit the road dived and she found this equally scary.

Several times they stopped to let other cars grind their way up, and at the valley bottom they began climbing again, the road even more steep and formidable than before.

'Hardknott Pass,' said Kiel. 'The road climbs one

inch in every three and a half. The steepest in England.
It was built by the Romans and on the other side are the
ruins of a fort. We'll stop there if you like.'

Terri nodded. She could not speak. Never in her life
had she experienced anything as hair-raising. Wrynose
had been bad enough, but this was worse. How the car
made it, she did not know. She wondered what would
happen if their brakes failed. It was a thought too
terrifying to voice.

'Are there any accidents up here?' she whispered.

He grinned. 'Not so much accidents as mechanical
failure—or human error—someone refusing to give
way, causing the whole line of traffic to snarl up,
jamming the pass for hours. It's almost a challenge to
everyone who comes to the Lakes to climb Hardknott
Pass. It's twelve thousand and ninety-one feet at the
top.'

When they reached the highest point and rounded
the tortuous bend to descend the other side it was only
faint relief. They stopped at the ruins and Terri got
out. Her legs were so shaky she was forced to cling to
Kiel for support. 'We don't have to go back that way?'

'Not if you don't want to. What's the matter? You
look as white as a ghost. You should try it when it's
dark—that's when it's time to worry.' He chuckled as
she recoiled.

'No, thanks,' she said, her imagination working
overtime.

They walked up to the fort's granite walls,
examining the stone foundations of the granary and
the headquarters. The fort was perched on a ledge
with the bath house below and the parade ground
above.

There was a gate that led to nowhere, right over the
cliff edge, and the scenery around the parade ground
was positively ferocious. Crags jutted out from steep

slopes which fell to the valley below, and apart from this large flat square there were boulders everywhere.

Eventually they left and began the last part of their descent. 'Didn't you enjoy that?' asked Kiel, when he finally stopped the car at Eskdale.

'It was certainly the experience you predicted,' said Terri, 'but I don't think I'd like to try it again in a hurry.'

'It will be a long drive home if we go all the way round.' His lips quirked.

'I don't care,' she said quickly, and he smiled.

'I think we've just time for a ride on the Ratty. That should be more to your liking.'

'The Ratty?' She frowned.

'A miniature railway,' he certified. 'It was constructed at the height of the Victorian industrial boom to carry iron ore from Eskdale to Ravensglass. In 1915 it was re-laid as a tourist attraction and is certainly a must while we're here.'

And so they paid their money and got on the train, each carriage highly polished and in immaculate working order.

'It runs all the year round,' Kiel told her, 'and as well as fun for tourists it's also the chief form of communication for people who live in the valley of Eskdale.'

This was one trip Terri was glad she hadn't missed. They steamed through leafy green glades, ran parallel with drystone walls, waved to the occupants of little grey cottages.

It was different, and crushed against Kiel's side in the tiny carriage she wished the ride would last for ever. She had never thought to enjoy his company so much after her hostile reception, and was glad of the long journey back. She wanted to prolong these special moments.

They had tea at a tiny farmhouse, and all this time Kiel made no attempt to touch her. But she was beginning to forget Barry's assault, and craved contact. He still excited her like no one else ever had.

Almost as though she had spoken her thoughts out loud he caught her hand as they came out of the farmhouse. 'It's been a long time since I had a complete day away from my work,' he remarked.

'I hope you're not regretting it?' A tiny frown creased her brow.

'Not in the least,' he assured her positively. 'And how about you? You certainly look happier. Have you quite got over your nasty experience?'

She nodded, smiling shyly, and he pulled her gently to him.

'I'm glad. I wouldn't like to say what I'd have done to Barry had his bestial actions had any long-lasting effect.'

Without Kiel they might have done. He had driven away her anxieties. He had filled her with an awareness of him instead, an entirely different sort of feeling.

Her arms slid involuntarily round his back as he pressed her to him and she tilted her chin, smiling up into his face. He lowered his head and kissed her brow gently. Then he held back a few inches and looked at her, judging her reaction. The next minute he pulled her roughly against him and his mouth devoured hers with a hunger that was equalled by her own mounting passion.

She had fought Barry off, but not this man. She wanted him with an intensity that frightened her, pressing herself ever closer, parting her lips to accept his kiss.

When he lifted his head and released her she felt disappointed. She wanted this kiss to go on and on.

She wanted to show him how much she cared. He was not doing it today as an experiment, he was doing it because he wanted to, she was sure.

'This is neither the time nor the place,' Kiel said quietly. 'I'm not used to being watched when I make love.'

Terri had not seen another car pull up, or its hungry occupants spill out and make their way to the tea-rooms, giving them smiling glances as they did so.

She felt a glow as she settled herself back in the car. Even the scenery took on a rosy hue. They stopped by one of the lakes and watched the sinking sun blaze a blood-red trail across the darkening waters. It was one of the most spectacular sights Terri had ever seen, and sharing it with Kiel added to her pleasure.

When they finally arrived back at his house it was dark. 'Thank you for a wonderful day,' she said.

'The pleasure's all mine,' he smiled. 'Let's get washed and changed and see what delights Mrs B's provided for supper. I don't know about you, but I'm starving!'

No sooner had they sat down to their meal, though, than he was called out. 'I'm sorry,' he said, looking angry. 'But I suppose I should be grateful we've had an uninterrupted day.'

When he had gone, Terri ate her supper, read for a while, and then made her way to bed. It had been a long and tiring day, sometimes hair-raising, mostly enjoyable. She wouldn't have missed it for anything.

In bed she lay listening for Kiel to return, but her eyes closed despite all her efforts to stay awake, and she knew nothing more until the early morning sun kissed her face. She sat up and stretched, smiling to herself. 'Good morning, sunshine,' she sang. Life felt very good at that moment.

She went over to the window, looking down at the

sparkling lake in the distance, the shadows of light and shade on the fells. It was perfectly clear this morning with none of the mist that frequently touched the mountains.

A solitary buzzard wheeled high above. Blackbirds and sparrows squabbled on the lawn. A great tit performed acrobatic feats in a nearby fir tree. Terri couldn't wait to begin another day.

After showering and donning a crisp green sundress, she ran downstairs. The table was laid but the dining-room empty. Mrs Barnes followed her in. 'Good morning, Miss Denning. The doctor's been called out. He said you're to have an idle day.'

'When's he coming back?' asked Terri eagerly.

Mrs Barnes shrugged. 'It's anyone's guess. Not usually until early evening. But with you here, who's to say?'

Terri hugged her warm thoughts to herself. She hoped he'd come back early. She really did. She ate a leisurely breakfast and then went outside into the warm sunshine. The mountains huddled together all around her, giant crags that had been split by centuries of frost and ice. Boulders spilled untidily. There were falling becks, catching the glint of the sun, and trees and shrubs hanging on to the higher slopes for dear life.

Lower down, grasses, heather and mosses struggled for survival against the extremes of weather to which they were exposed. Drystone walls crawled inexorably over the landscape, and in a hollow a tiny farmhouse sat all alone.

A dog barked in the distance, the loud liquid notes of a tiny wren came from nearby, and then the drone of a car's engine, and Terri pricked her ears, wondering who was coming this way.

Her heart skittered at the thought that it might be

D

Kiel, but it was not the long white car that swung into view, it was her own little red Mini. There was still a chance it might be Kiel, though. He might have brought it for her.

She ran across the lawn, a smile of greeting gentling her face, but it faded abruptly when Barry eased himself out of the Mini and walked towards her. For the first time in her life, she was not pleased to see him.

CHAPTER SIX

BARRY looked contrite, his eyes sad, his mouth down-turned. 'What can I say? I'm truly sorry for what happened.'

Terri eyed him scornfully. 'Being sorry won't help. I've realised that Kiel's right about you. I just never saw that side of you before—and I hope I never see it again.'

'You won't,' he assured her. 'I won't ever force myself on you again, I promise.'

'But why did you do it at all?' Terri was careful to keep a good distance between them. Even the sight of Barry turned her stomach over. And did he really imagine that apologising would put things right? It would be a long time, if ever, before she forgave him.

'Because,' he said slowly, 'you're irresistible. You're no longer my old mate's sister, but a beauty in your own right.'

'And that makes a difference? It gives you a right to—to attack me?' she thrust fiercely, the purple of her eyes glowing like jewels in the sunlight.

He shook his head, his face screwed up in pain. 'Not attack you, Terri. I never meant to attack you. But I've seen you in a new light. I don't want what happened to spoil things between us. I want to——'

'It already has,' cut in Terri coldly. 'Can't you see that? We'll never get back on the same footing.'

He looked down at his hands. 'I don't want that same footing, Terri. I want you to be my—er—girl-friend.'

She stared at him aghast, unable to take in what he was saying. 'Isn't Laura your girl?'

Barry shrugged, his lips twisting wryly. 'Laura doesn't mean anything to me.'

'But you don't waste an opportunity to go and see her. What is it, Barry, a purely physical relationship? How disgusting!'

He snorted angrily, his face darkening. 'Kiel's been poisoning your mind, I see.'

'I never believed him before,' she said, tossing her head haughtily. 'But now I do. Perhaps it was purely the drink, but whatever caused your appalling behaviour, it's ruined our relationship.'

'It needn't,' he said cajolingly. 'It won't happen again.' He tried to take her hands, but she backed away in alarm.

'Don't touch me!'

He swung away in self-disgust. 'Was it that bad?'

'You know it was,' she cried. 'Surely you remember? You were like an animal. I shall never forget what you did to me—never!'

Barry hung his head. 'It's the drink,' he admitted. 'I can never remember what I've done, but I'm told it completely alters my character.'

'So why drink?' Terri demanded.

He shrugged. 'One has to be sociable.'

'Meaning you don't want to stop?' she demanded scathingly. 'Kiel said you had.'

'I don't drink so much,' he said defensively, 'but it's one of my pleasures in life.'

'It will ruin you,' she accused.

'Who's told you that—Kiel? Seems to me you're getting mighty pally with him all of a sudden.'

'And if I am?' She tilted her chin and looked at him challengingly.

'You're a fool. Kiel's not the marrying sort.'

Her head jerked. 'Who's talking about marriage? I've only known him a few days.'

'You wouldn't be staying here if you weren't seriously interested,' sneered Barry.

'I've done nothing to be ashamed of,' Terri said sharply. 'Nothing at all has happened between us.'

He eyed her stonily. 'And how long do you intend remaining? Until Kiel finds another nurse, or until he tires of you?'

'You make me sick!' snapped Terri. 'I don't have to explain my actions to you nor anybody. But if you must know, I'm enjoying it here, it's a very beautiful place, and I see no reason why I shouldn't make the most of my stay.'

He did not look pleased, his eyes expressing his disgust. Then the next second he smiled. 'But Kiel's not here now, is he? So why not spend the day with me?'

He had a nerve! thought Terri. Did he really think she would go out with him, after what he had done? She shook her head. 'I'm sorry, it wouldn't work.'

He frowned angrily. 'You mean you don't trust me any more?'

Terri shrugged. 'I don't feel comfortable. It's gone, that rapport we had. I'm sorry, Barry, but I can't wipe out what you did. I don't think I shall ever forget it.'

His lips clamped and he stood for a moment glowering. 'So that's the way it's going to be. One momentary indiscretion and I'm in disgrace for the rest of my life. Are you going to complain to Richard?'

'I shan't say anything to my brother,' she said with quiet dignity. 'But I'd be obliged if you don't come visiting when I'm around.'

Barry shoved his hands into his pockets and tried to look unconcerned, though the pulse working in his jaw told her otherwise. 'Would it put you out if I asked for a lift back to the flat?' he said quietly.

What could she say? It would be churlish to refuse. She nodded. 'I'll let Mrs Barnes know where I'm going.'

When she returned to the car, he was in the passenger seat. She slid in beside him and he was glumly silent during the drive. It was not until they were almost there that he said, 'You're being very hard on me, Terri, for one small mistake on my part.'

'Small!' she exclaimed shrilly. 'I don't call what you did small. Do you know what would have happened if Kiel hadn't walked in?'

'I wouldn't have gone that far,' he mumbled self-consciously.

'Wouldn't you?' she cried. 'You didn't know what you were doing. I'm sorry, Barry, I don't want to discuss the subject again. I feel deeply hurt, deeply humiliated, that you should take advantage of our friendship. Because that's what I thought you were— my friend. I was proud of our relationship. It was good. Now it's ruined. I'm not sure I even want to see you again.'

'Terri!' He sounded distraught. 'You have my word that I won't lay another finger on you.'

'I won't give you the chance!'

'You're so hard,' he complained.

'Am I?' She cast him an oblique glance. 'Kiel was right when he said all you wanted from me was an affair.'

His lips thinned. 'He had no right to discuss me.'

'He only says what he thinks is the truth.'

'And you believe him?'

She nodded. 'I have no reason not to, not now. You've proved him right. I can't think why you stay here when there's so much animosity between you.'

'I'm beginning to think it's time I went,' he agreed bitterly. 'I've given it a fair trial, but it's not going to work. I only joined Kiel because it was what my father wished.'

'He'll be hurt, then, if you leave?' Barry nodded. 'So why don't you start your own practice? It's the obvious solution.'

'You think I haven't thought of that?' he demanded loudly. 'There's just one small thing stopping me. Money! I could certainly never raise anything like enough to set up on my own.'

'How did Kiel manage?' she asked.

'Kiel's got the Midas touch,' he rasped.

'Or is it that he believes in working whereas you prefer the company of a pretty girl, given a choice?'

'He's really brainwashed you, hasn't he?' sneered Barry. 'I'm nothing in your eyes now.'

'You did a pretty good job of convincing me yourself,' said Terri, applying her brakes, relieved they had finally arrived and so put an end to the conversation.

He got out and she would have driven away had he not put his head back into the car. 'How about lunch, for old times' sake?'

Terri shook her head in reply. 'I told Mrs Barnes I'd be back.'

As she restarted the Mini, Kiel's car came to a halt in front of her. Terri's face lit up, her heart beating a tattoo of recognition. But he frowned harshly. 'What the devil are you doing here?'

She was shocked by the tight anger in his voice.

'Barry brought my car. I've just dropped him off.' She bit her lip anxiously. What was happening to the harmony they had built up?

'After what he did to you?' His eyes were steely.

'He was very apologetic.'

'I bet he was! He's good at that. Promises it won't happen again—until the next time.'

Although Terri had not, and never would, forgive Barry, she could not dismiss their years of friendship so easily. 'I think being tied down here has a lot to do with his restlessness, ' she said.

'If he wants to leave, he can,' grated Kiel, 'and good riddance.'

'Then why don't you persuade his father? Barry doesn't want to stay here any more than you want to have him.'

'He's been whingeing on your shoulder?' he asked angrily.

'No, but I understand Barry. It's easy to see that he's dissatisfied. I suggested he ought to start his own practice.'

Kiel snorted. 'He'd never make a go of it. He hasn't the staying power.'

'You mean he's never had the chance? You admitted yourself he never lets his private life interfere with his work.'

'Quite a little do-gooder, aren't you?' he snarled. 'If you feel so strongly about it, why don't you join him? It seems to me I made the wrong decision when I took you away from here. I thought I was doing you a favour. Little did I know you'd come back for more. You make me sick.'

Terri trembled with rage because Kiel wouldn't listen, and disappointment because the affinity they had built up yesterday had disintegrated before her eyes.

She shook her head wildly. 'That's not right. I was grateful for your intervention and I've not forgiven Barry, but——'

'But nothing,' growled Kiel. 'Go and collect your things and then do what the hell you like. I don't want to see you again—ever.'

Terri knew there was no point in arguing. Kiel meant every word he said. His grey eyes were hard, his face set into a mask of contempt.

She gave him one last pleading look before driving away. Not that it did any good. He might have been made of stone for all the emotion she saw there. Her brief interlude was over, and all she could do now was go home.

Her heart was as heavy as lead as she drove back to Kiel's house. Mrs Barnes had lunch waiting and Terri dutifully ate some of it, even though every mouthful choked her.

'I'm going back to London as soon as I've packed,' she announced.

The housekeeper frowned. 'Dr Braden didn't tell me. I was under the impression you'd be here for several days?'

Terri shrugged. 'I was going to stay until he found a replacement, but he's asked me to leave now.'

Mrs Barnes frown deepened. 'You're his new nurse? I didn't realise, I thought you were a friend. He's never brought a girl here before. I really thought you were someone special.'

How Terri wished she was! She had felt things were going that way yesterday, but it had been shortlived. Their day out was now nothing more than a precious memory.

'I'm afraid not,' she said ruefully.

There was a lump in her throat as she left the house. She had phoned Richard and told him she was returning, but given no details except that it hadn't worked out.

Her route took her past the surgery and Barry was standing outside. She slowed and stopped.

'I've been waiting for you,' he said. 'Kiel had no right telling you to go. You've done no wrong.' There was an angry frown on his face as he opened her door. 'Hell, I don't see why you should do what he says. Hop out, I'm going to take you for a drive.'

Terri's first and immediate thought was that he still planned to seduce her, then she cast the idea out as unworthy. Barry had promised nothing like that would happen again—and she believed him. But still she hesitated. 'Richard's expecting me. I really ought to go.'

'You're not staying in the Lakes, then?'

She shook her head. 'This place has suddenly lost its attraction.'

He compressed his lips ruefully. 'And I'm partly to blame. But surely you don't begrudge me an hour of your company? That's all I ask. Who knows when we'll see each other again?'

Terri found it difficult to refuse. She had known Barry so long it was almost as if what had happened was a bad dream. Certainly there was nothing in his behaviour now to suggest he had any ulterior motive— and she really didn't feel up to the long drive home.

So she scrambled out of her Mini and into his car. They had driven for about fifteen minutes when he said, 'How would you like to meet my father?'

It was such an unexpected question that Terri could only stare.

'He and my stepmother live a couple of minutes' drive from here, that's all,' he explained. 'Kiel enthused so much about the Lake District that they retired here. I usually try to visit them once a week.'

'I hardly think it's right you should take me,' said Terri.

'Why not?' he frowned. 'They know all about you. I've spoken of you and Richard so often they'll be more than pleased to meet you.'

Without waiting for her answer he forked off the

main road and they came upon a sleepy little hamlet with not a soul in sight. He stopped at a Lakeland-slated cottage on the outskirts.

They walked up a narrow crazy-paved path, hemmed on either side with sweet-scented roses. The door stood open, letting in the warm summer sunshine. Inside there were brasses and hand-made rugs. It smelt of polish and more roses, and Terri felt immediately at home.

Barry called out and his stepmother appeared. She was well-built and tall with thinning mousy hair, and probably in her late sixties, though she looked so fit and well it was difficult to put an age on her. She wore gold-rimmed spectacles and a charming smile. 'Barry! How lovely! We didn't expect you today. And who's this?' Her smile enveloped Terri as well.

'Terri Denning,' said Barry. 'Richard's sister.'

'Oh, yes,' said Pamela Allen at once. 'Barry told us you'd come to work here. How nice of you to visit us.'

Her eyes were Kiel's eyes. This was his mother. It was uncanny looking at someone so much like him.

'Unfortunately,' said Barry, 'Kiel's decided she's not suitable.'

'What a pity!' exclaimed the woman. 'All this way for nothing. It was a bit naughty of Kiel to say he'd employ you and then change his mind. That's not like him. I——' She broke off as her husband came into the room.

Although Kiel looked like his mother, Barry did not take after his father. There was no similarity between the two men. Mr Allen was slight, with a shock of steel-grey hair and a lined, interesting face.

'Father,' said Barry at once. 'How are you?'

'As well as they'll let me be,' smiled the man. 'Can't grumble.'

Barry turned to Terri. 'This is Terri Denning.'

James Allen held out his hand. 'Nice to meet you. How's the new job?' Terri liked the warmth and strength of his grasp.

'Kiel's decided she's not suitable,' said Pamela for her.

'So I'm afraid I'm off back to London,' added Terri ruefully.

He frowned. 'Not today?'

She nodded.

'Then you should be well on your way, unless, of course, you like driving through the night. Not that I don't appreciate you coming to see us, but——'

'It's my fault,' cut in Barry. 'I'm afraid I insisted.'

'Typical!' snorted his father. 'But now you're here you may as well stay and have a cup of tea. Put the kettle on, Pamela. We'll go out into the garden. The roses are beautiful this year.'

Barry smiled at Terri. 'My father's a keen rose grower. Everyone has to look at his roses.'

They were indeed a magnificent display, and after dutifully admiring them they gathered round the table on the patio.

Time passed so quickly that Terri cried out in dismay when she discovered it was nearly five. 'I must go—Richard will be frantic! Can I phone and tell him I got delayed?'

'I have a better idea,' said Mrs Allen. 'Why don't you stay the night and make an early start in the morning?'

'Oh, I couldn't,' said Terri at once. 'I mean—well, you don't know me.'

'You're a friend of Barry's, that's good enough for us.'

Terri shook her head, bemused. 'You're so kind. I must admit I don't fancy setting off now.'

'Then there's no argument,' said Mrs Allen, looking

pleased. 'In fact, if you've nothing to rush home for why not spend a few days with us? Maybe it will help make up for your disappointment?'

'It would be an imposition,' cried Terri, even though the idea was tempting.

'Imposition my foot!' said James. 'Tell her, Barry.'

Barry smiled. 'They really mean it.'

'And how about you, Barry?' added his father. 'Can you wangle some time off?'

He shook his head. 'But I'll come next weekend.'

Terri felt she had no choice. The odds were against her. They were dear people, though, and she knew she would enjoy herself.

'It's settled,' said Pamela delightedly.

Then Terri remembered that her case was still in her car.

'I'll fetch it,' said Barry when she explained her predicament. 'I'll go now. I'll be back before you've even noticed I've gone.'

He had left before it occurred to her that she ought to have gone with him and brought her car here. It would be a certain giveaway to Kiel that she had not left the district. How stupid she was!

In Barry's absence, she phoned Richard. He was all for her staying as long as she liked, and she guessed he had not been too happy at the thought of her invading them.

Within an hour Barry was back. 'Was Kiel there?' she asked anxiously when he came into the room.

He shook his head.

Mrs Allen was quick to read Terri's tension. 'You're wondering what my son will say about you coming to stay with us? He'll be delighted, I'm sure. He mustn't have liked telling you there was no job after all. It's the least we can do.'

It was bedtime before Barry finally left. It had been

a pleasant evening with no hint of the man who had violated her body. He was the Barry she knew and loved.

Her bedroom was tiny, but comfortable, with a patchwork quilt and rag rugs. Pamela Allen was a natural homemaker.

As she went to sleep Terri's thoughts were on Kiel, what his reaction would be when he discovered where she was.

When she woke the next morning Terri could see nothing through the window except the sky and treetops, with white wispy clouds drifting lazily by.

She caught the shrill of a child's voice from the village, the undisputed chorus of bird-song, and unable to lie there a moment longer collected her towel and toothbrush and went along to the bathroom.

Here again were signs of Mrs Allen's handiwork in the form of crocheted bathmats. She clearly loved her little cottage. Terri envied her serenity, her peace of mind. At the moment she felt as though there would never be peace for herself again. It was a silly thought, she knew that time healed everything, but she felt that the pain in her heart would stay with her for the rest of her life.

When she went downstairs Pamela Allen was busy in the kitchen. The woman looked happy. 'I've had a phone call from Kiel. He's coming over later. Isn't that lovely? It's so long since I've seen him.'

'Does he know I'm here?' asked Terri quickly, feeling a sense of doom.

Her hostess looked vague. 'He didn't say, but I should imagine so. Barry will have told him.'

Barry would have had it dragged out of him, thought Terri, and that was the reason Kiel was coming. She hated involving these lovely people in her private argument, but without her car, she was stuck here.

She would have to face Kiel, face his wrath in front of his parents, bear her embarrassment as best she could. Perhaps she ought to warn his mother what was likely to happen?

But how could she say Kiel was sending her home because he didn't approve of her relationship with Barry? The whole sorry story would come out. She had no idea whether they knew about Barry's split personality. They knew he wasn't a worker, but did they know about his many affairs? It was a difficult situation and she was not sure she could handle it.

'You don't look pleased,' said Pamela. 'Don't worry, I know how you feel. I'll give him a piece of my mind. He had no right turning you away.'

'Please,' said Terri quickly, 'I'd rather you didn't. He'll think I've complained.'

'Never fear,' said Pamela, 'I can handle my son.'

This wasn't what Terri was afraid of, it was the reprisal. His mother might not know how hard and cruel Kiel could be. But at least she had been forewarned. She would have time to condition herself.

They had breakfast on the patio and then Terri washed up and tidied the kitchen while Mrs Allen flicked imaginary specks of dust from the furniture and chased the vacuum cleaner round the rooms. Then they all sat outside drinking endless cups of tea, Mr Allen darting off every now and then to inspect his roses. Terri had one ear attuned for Kiel's car.

They were in the middle of a cold buffet lunch when he arrived. He stopped short as he came into the room. 'You!' he stabbed, looking straight at Terri. 'What are you doing here?'

Before she could speak Pamela Allen said, 'She's our guest. Barry brought her.'

'Did he, by jove?' Kiel's eyes narrowed angrily.

'That's right,' added his stepfather. 'And we felt sorry for her, so she's staying for a few days.'

'Been giving you a sob story, has she?' asked Kiel coldly.

'Nothing of the sort,' said his mother quickly. 'Sit down and join us. I expected you earlier.'

'I've been having a talk with Barry—but he didn't tell me Teresa was here.'

Good for Barry, thought Terri, but she could imagine how heated the conversation must have been.

'I wonder why he didn't tell you?' frowned Pamela.

'Because he knew I wouldn't approve,' snapped Kiel.

'But why?' insisted his mother.

Kiel flicked her an impatient glance. 'It's far too long a story. Let's forget it.' He drew up a chair between Terri and his mother, helping himself to a selection of cold meats.

Terri was very aware of his nearness, the magnetism that always rushed from him to her. She found it difficult to eat, picking at her food, wondering why life had become so complicated all of a sudden.

Conversation inevitably got around to Kiel's work. 'I suppose,' he said, giving Terri a daggered look, 'she's expanded on her theory that Barry ought to start up his own practice?'

James Allen raised thick white brows. 'Is that what Barry wants? He's not said anything to me.'

Terri glanced at Kiel defiantly. 'Barry would jump at the opportunity, provided he had the financial backing.'

'Is that so?' Mr Allen's eyes lit up.

Kiel shook his head angrily. 'Don't plough your money into something that's a guaranteed loser, James. Barry hasn't the staying power.'

'I don't know,' said the older man slowly. 'Perhaps he's ready to settle down now. He's worked with you, what do you think?'

Reluctantly Kiel said, 'I've no complaints, he's a good doctor, but given an excuse to have an hour off and he will.'

'But surely,' said James, 'that's because he's working with you? I'm not stupid, I know the two of you don't get on. If he was on his own it would be different. He'd have to knuckle under. I don't think he'd jeopardise his career.'

'He'd make a go of it, I know he would, if he were on his own,' insisted Terri.

Kiel flung her an arrogant look. 'And what interest have you in all this? Would you want to work for him, is that it? Are you looking for a job for yourself?'

'Kiel!' admonished Pamela sharply.

But he ignored his mother. 'Is that it?' he persisted. 'Is that the real reason you persuaded him to bring you here, to get my parents on your side? They already know that your friendship with Barry goes back a long way, but do they know exactly what sort of relationship you have?'

Terri tilted her chin, trying to ignore the swift colour that flooded her cheeks. 'You're being unfair, Kiel!'

'Am I?' Mockery flared in his eyes.

'My personal relationship with Barry has nothing to do with it,' she said tightly.

'That's right,' put in his mother. 'They're good friends, and why shouldn't they be?'

'Friends?' asked Kiel sceptically.

His mother shrugged. 'Well, if they're more than friends, what does it matter? I like Terri. I think she'd make Barry a good wife.'

'Wife?' thundered Kiel. 'You're living with your head in the clouds, Mother!'

'Well, maybe they do things differently these days. I don't say I'd approve of them living together, but I wouldn't exactly forbid it.'

Kiel's tone softened. 'I doubt it will come to that.'

'Then I don't know what you're talking about.'

'Teresa does,' said Kiel, 'and I think she's getting the message good and clear.' His voice was hard and bitter, and full of venom.

Terri had never felt so uncomfortable in her life. Kiel was making it impossible for her to stay. He resented her getting on so well with his parents. In fact he did not want her in the Lake District at all. She wished she had never let Barry persuade her to come here.

'Enough of this double talk,' said James sternly. 'I'll have a word with Barry myself. You're biased, Kiel, and it's easy to see you're transferring your animosity to Terri.'

The conversation turned to less personal matters, but even so there was still an atmosphere, and Terri was glad when the meal was over and Kiel went out into the garden with his stepfather.

'I don't know what's got into Kiel,' said Pamela over the washing up. 'It's odd he should take his dislike of Barry out on you.'

Terri shrugged. 'I'd prefer not to discuss it, Mrs Allen.'

The woman smiled sympathetically. 'Whatever you do, don't let him upset you. As soon as he's gone you can settle down to a restful few days.'

But in this assumption Pamela was wrong. At dinner Kiel announced his intention of staying overnight. And Terri knew it was deliberate, that he intended making things as unpleasant as possible so that she would leave.

When the telephone rang Kiel said, 'I'll get it.' But within seconds he was back, a scowl darkening his brow. 'It's for you, Teresa.'

Her eyes widened questioningly.

'Barry,' he announced sharply.

Terri squirmed inwardly and closed the door carefully behind her. 'Hello, Barry,' she said brightly, more brightly than she felt.

'What's Kiel doing there?' he demanded at once.

'He turned up for lunch. At first I thought you'd told him about me, but then——'

'Do you really think I'd do that?' he interrupted loudly. 'I put your car in the garage so he wouldn't know you were still around. He must have guessed.'

'No,' she said quickly. 'He didn't know until he got here. His face was a picture when he saw me, but now he's announced that he's staying overnight.'

'The devil he has!' Barry sounded cross. 'It's because of you—it has to be. Watch him, Terri, he's planning something. I'll bring your car over first thing in the morning and then ask him to run me back. He'll have no excuse for staying any longer.'

'I wish you would,' she said. 'And I wish I knew what was going on in his mind. I'm sure he resents me being here, resents the fact that I'm getting on so well with your family. It's a most unfortunate situation.'

'And it's my fault.' He sounded rueful. 'Seems I'm always getting you into trouble.'

'You weren't to know,' she said at once. 'It was a million to one chance his turning up here.'

He sighed. 'I'll see you tomorrow, then. I only rang to make sure you'd settled in.'

'I would have done, if it hadn't been for Kiel,' she replied sadly. 'Your parents are dears, though. They're really making me feel at home.'

'I knew they would. Good night, Terri.'

'Thanks, Barry.' It was amazing how she had almost forgotten the ugly scene at the flat. Barry in this mood was the best friend any girl could have.

Back in the sitting-room all eyes turned expectantly towards her. She smiled self-consciously. 'He just wanted to know if I was all right. He's bringing my car over in the morning. Perhaps you'll give him a lift back, Kiel?'

'Sorry,' he said coolly, 'but I've decided to stay on for a few days. That's if you'll have me, Mother? He can manage without me.'

CHAPTER SEVEN

PAMELA beamed joyously at her son. 'Lovely!'

James nodded his agreement, but Terri knew the real reason for Kiel's decision. She did not know what he was afraid of, but he was going to stay until he had got rid of her.

'If you'll excuse me,' she said, feeling a sudden need to escape, 'I'd like to go to bed. It must be the country air—I'm exhausted. Good night, everyone.'

In her room she stood looking out at the flower-filled garden. It was still light, far too early for bed. And she wasn't tired. It had been an excuse; she'd had to get away from the cloying atmosphere of Kiel's presence.

She really could not weigh him up. He had shown an interest in her when they first met, and again when she stayed at his house. There had been the stirrings of mutual attraction. She had thought something would develop from it, that it would build into a deeper more meaningful relationship.

So why had he changed? Wasn't she allowed to forgive Barry? Or did he hate himself for weakening sufficiently to show interest? Did he intend making sure it wouldn't happen again by getting rid of her?

If that was the case, Barry coming tomorrow would add fuel to his fire. Inadvertently, by telephoning, Barry had convinced Kiel there was something between them. She could deny it all she liked, Kiel would never believe her now.

Eventually she undressed and climbed into bed, but she lay a long time listening to the murmur of voices below, her heart stopping when she heard Kiel's footsteps on the stairs.

She knew it was him, she was vitally conscious of everything about him. That he despised her made no difference to the way she felt—the awareness, the racing of her pulses every time he drew near.

Last night she had slept easily, but with Kiel in the house she tossed and turned. Tomorrow he would begin his campaign. She did not know whether she could take it. Nor was it fair on his parents. They had asked for none of this. They had invited her to stay out of the kindness of their hearts. They didn't want their lives disrupted by Kiel's unreasonable behaviour.

Yet there was nothing she could do about it. He revelled in what he was doing, he actually enjoyed humiliating her, and he would go on doing it for as long as it took to get her out.

When Terri went downstairs the next morning Kiel and his father had already breakfasted and were out in the garden. 'He's explaining some of the finer points of rose growing,' laughed Pamela, 'as though he hasn't told him a hundred times already.' She looked at Terri closely. 'You look a little peaky.'

She lifted her shoulders. 'I didn't sleep too well.' She was very much aware of the purple shadows beneath her eyes, even her carefully applied make-up failed to disguise them.

'Then it's a lazy day for you,' said Pamela.

'But I can't let you do all the work, it wouldn't be fair.'

'You're here to relax and enjoy yourself,' returned the older woman strongly. 'Make the most of it.'

How could she, with Kiel here? He was the most disturbing man she had ever met. It was ironic that she had to fall in love with someone who did not return her feelings. If only she could love Michael there would be no problem. Michael had always loved her, swore he would never change. Now she knew how he felt. It was agony.

Mrs Allen joined Terri for a cup of tea, chatting about an item of news she had heard on the radio. 'How's your brother?' she asked, when she had exhausted the subject. 'Hasn't he just got married?'

Terri nodded. 'He's very happy. I wish I didn't have to go back and intrude on them. But until I find a place of my own, I have no option.'

'I know what newlyweds are like,' agreed the other woman. 'It's such a pity things haven't worked out here. Why is it, do you think? I can't understand Kiel offering you the job and then telling you there isn't one when you get here.'

'To tell you the truth,' admitted Terri, 'he thinks Barry is the reason I came.'

'I see,' said Pamela slowly, 'now I'm beginning to understand. The boys have never seen eye to eye, I'll admit, and the way Kiel was talking last night I knew something was wrong. I'm glad you've told me. But don't rush back to London. Feel free to stay as long as you like. James and I abhor these constant hostilities between our two children. We do our best to ignore them.'

She sighed and continued, 'It's a clash of personalities, I'm afraid. Kiel's father was so different from James. He was a very volatile man, never afraid to speak his own mind, no matter to whom. Kiel takes after him. He'll flare up at the slightest provocation, and just because Barry's got a completely different attitude towards life, Kiel holds it against him.'

'And I'm in the thick of it,' said Terri. 'I wish Barry had warned me. I never even knew he had a stepbrother. I had no idea Dr Braden and he were related.'

'I think,' said Pamela slowly, 'it might be a good idea Barry setting up on his own. James and I were discussing it in bed last night. Originally we'd hoped they'd form a proper partnership, but now we can see they're as much at each other's throats as ever. The trouble is Barry's never been as ambitious as Kiel. Kiel always wanted to be someone, to be at the top. He has plans, though he never discusses them with us.'

She stopped and grinned ruefully. 'I'm going on a bit, aren't I? I'm sorry. It's not often I get on my high horse.' She pushed her chair from the table. 'Let's get these things washed up and go outside. Barry's not coming until after lunch, by the way. Kiel phoned him.'

Terri could imagine the friction that must have caused and was glad she did not have the opportunity to talk to Kiel alone, for she would definitely have given him a piece of her mind. He was being grossly unfair about the whole situation.

When Barry did arrive, the atmosphere was unbearable; the hostility between the two brothers had never been more pronounced. She was glad when James took Barry out into the garden.

'What are you thinking?' Kiel's deep voice interrupted her contemplation.

She closed her eyes and lay back on the lounger. 'Nothing that need concern you.'

'You were eyeing Barry very intently. What do you think he and James are discussing?'

Terri shrugged. 'It's no business of mine.'

'But you think it might be about Barry setting up on his own?'

'You started the ball rolling, not me.' She looked at him coldly.

'Meaning to say you wouldn't have mentioned it,

even though it is a way of getting yourself a job—and remaining with Barry?'

She shook her head. 'I could hardly voice my opinion in a stranger's house.'

'But you had no such misgivings about telling me.'

'You're different.'

'Am I? You've not known me long. I'm still a virtual stranger.'

'I've known you long enough to have formed an opinion,' she said tightly.

'Not a good enough one, judging by the way you're still clinging to Barry.' His lips were thin and he frowned crossly.

Terri turned her head away impatiently. 'It's not like that. He's apologised and I've accepted it. We're friends again, that's all.'

'I prefer to use my eyes,' said Kiel. 'I trust my own intuition.'

'And you're never wrong?' What a pointless conversation this was! He would never admit that he had misjudged either of them, so why didn't he shut up?

'Not normally.'

'You're wrong about Barry,' she snapped, 'Barry and me.'

'Time will tell,' he growled savagely.

She caught a glimpse of Pamela watching them through the open kitchen window, a frown on her face. 'Your mother's got her eye on us,' she told him.

'My mother doesn't tell me what to do, even though she'd like to,' he snarled.

'I think you should be a little more respectful in her house,' she said evenly. 'It's not fair to cause unpleasantness when she's been kind enough to ask me to stay.'

'Are you daring to tell me what I should or should

not do?' He leaned forward, his grey eyes burning into her, compelling her to look at him.

Terri quivered beneath his gaze, amazed that at a time like this she could still feel such awareness. He was even more overpowering when he was angry, sending a strange thrill of feverish excitement through her limbs.

But she managed to inject just the right amount of coldness into her voice. 'I can't stay here if this atmosphere continues, and that's what you want, isn't it? You don't like the fact that I'm getting on so well with your parents. You don't want me involved with your family.'

He looked impatient. 'Not my parents, I don't mind that. It's Barry. You're a disruptive influence on him. I think——'

At that moment his mother came out of the house bearing a tray of iced drinks. Her husband and Barry joined them and there was no further opportunity for private discussion.

Nor did she manage to talk to Barry alone—Kiel made sure of that. In fact Kiel did not leave her side until James got out the car to take Barry home. Then he took a stroll into the village, declaring he needed to replenish his stock of cigars. He had timed it perfectly, thought Terri bitterly.

'Well,' said Pamela, settling herself down in a chair. 'It's been a pleasant day, don't you think? It's rare we have both our sons home together and for once there were no sparks flying. Although I thought things still seemed a bit strained between you and Kiel.'

'Aren't they always?' said Terri.

'It's a pity,' Pamela said, 'because if you and Barry do—er—settle down together, I should hate there to be any unpleasantness.'

'Mrs Allen,' said Terri at once, knowing she must

clear up this misunderstanding before it went too far, 'Barry and I are just friends, that's all. We always have been. He's never treated me as anything but a sister.' She felt justified in uttering this white lie.

'Oh, I'm sorry,' said the woman. 'I really thought— I mean, when he brought you here, the way he looks at you. But—well, I'm sorry if I've got it wrong. I hope I haven't embarrassed you.'

Terri shook her head. 'Of course you haven't. I suppose it was natural you'd think that way. Kiel believes it too. In fact, he refuses to accept that there's nothing between Barry and me.'

'And he doesn't approve?' Pamela frowned. 'I know he's never approved of Barry's girl-friends in the past—he's picked up some pretty weird types—but you're different. I can't understand Kiel. Although he's my son I'm beginning to think I don't know him at all.'

Terri agreed. Kiel's behaviour was unpredictable. She did not think she would ever know where she stood with him.

'Something else,' said his mother, 'he's never stayed overnight here before. I can only think it's because you're here. He certainly made sure Barry had no opportunity to talk to you.'

'You noticed?'

'It was obvious.' Pamela paused and listened. 'I think that's him now.'

He walked into the room, smiling at the two women. 'It's a lovely evening. How about a stroll, Teresa? You won't sleep again tonight if you don't take some exercise.'

So he had noticed the shadows beneath her eyes and guessed at the reason. But did he know that it was he who was the cause of her restlessness, and not Barry? She thought not.

'A good suggestion, Kiel.' Pamela looked at Terri with a challenging gleam in her eyes.

And Terri knew she would not refuse. Any moments spent with Kiel, especially when he was in an amenable mood, were a rare treat. Despite his behaviour her feelings had not changed. She might tell herself that she hated him, that she hated his attitude, hated the way he treated her, but deep down inside there was still that warm glowing feeling whenever he came near.

He still had the power to excite her, to create an inner exhilaration. She would never forget the feel of his mouth on hers, the passion behind his kisses when she had turned liquid in his arms, her whole body on fire.

'Thank you, Kiel,' she said. 'I think I'd like that.'

They headed away from the village, walking slowly side by side. Despite the inches that separated them, Terri was as aware of him as if she was held in his arms. Her stomach was a chaos of emotion, her pulses racing all out of time with themselves. She was quite sure he felt no such reaction, and when she dared glance at him his face was set in thoughtful lines.

A narrow track led off the main road and he took it. There was not room here to walk side by side, so Terri followed a few paces behind, seizing the opportunity to study him.

He had a relaxed, loose-limbed stride, yet carried himself tall. His shoulders were broad and muscular, his waist and hips narrow, trousers moulding the firm length of thigh. His tawny hair lifted with the warm evening breeze and when he turned to look at her a smile curved the corners of his mouth.

She had not realised that her own steps had slowed, and she had fallen further and further behind, until he held out his hand and she hurried forward to slip her own into it.

The electric quality of his touch made her jerk away. It was like a shock wave, burning her, frightening her, but his fingers tightened and there was no escape.

The path climbed steadily, although Terri did not notice. She was aware only of the man at her side. She drew her strength from him, her feet light, almost as if she were walking on air.

When he stopped and they looked back she could see his parents' cottage like a doll's house far below. They were in a world of their own up here. His motive for bringing her was obscure, but that did not matter. The friction had gone.

Lakeland in miniature spread out in front of them and in Terri's heightened emotional state it was like nothing she had seen before. It was achingly beautiful and it was impossible not to be moved by it.

Kiel let go of her hand, but she could feel his very tangible presence and when he draped an arm loosely about her shoulders she could not stem the inevitable tensing of her muscles. She stopped breathing for several seconds, poised motionless on the brink of dizzy desire.

It was madness, when he had no feelings for her, when all he cared about was sending her back to Richard. Guiding her up here tonight was a devious tactic. She would never know how his mind worked, but she knew for a fact that he was not touching her for any emotional reasons. He did not feel as she did. Any moment now would come the punch line—the real reason he had invited her out.

And she was not disappointed. 'About Barry,' he began.

'What about him?' Her eyes flashed a sudden,

brilliant purple. 'I don't want to hear anything about Barry. I know your feelings on that score.'

'You don't know what I'm going to say,' he said equably.

'What you've said a dozen times before—that he's no good for me—or is it that I'm no good for him?' Her moments of happiness had been shortlived.

Kiel shook his head. 'I'm not talking about your relationship at all. It's your suggestion that he starts up on his own.'

'Don't tell me,' she spat. 'I know you'll do every thing in your power to put a stop to it. You really do hate the sight of him, don't you?'

'He's never given me any reason to like him,' said Kiel patiently. 'But when you had faith in him, despite what he'd done to you, I began to wonder whether there wasn't some good in him after all. Either that— or you're as bad as he is.'

Terri tilted her head and looked at him, bleeding inside. 'What are you trying to say?'

'I've been talking to James and he says that Barry is really keen on the idea. It amazes me. He's always taken the easy way out of everything. I told him it's jolly hard work and a long uphill grind when you're working for yourself, but he said that didn't bother him.'

'So you've given him your blessing? How big of you!' Terri did not feel the elation she should have done. 'Is James backing him?'

'As a matter of fact,' said Kiel, 'I am. James wanted to, but I've persuaded him that I'm in a better position.'

Terri swallowed hard and stared at him for a long moment. Had she misjudged him? This was something she had never expected.

'Of course it will be a strict business deal,' he

continued, 'and he'll have to pay me back—with interest.'

Some of her pleasure faded. 'Trust you to try and make something out of it! You'd do no one a good turn.'

His lips thinned. 'Is that what you think?'

She nodded.

'As a matter of fact,' he said, 'Barry was prepared to go elsewhere to borrow the money—just to prove he can go it alone. But in that event he'd have to start paying back straight away. Until he's established he'd find that extremely difficult, so I've agreed to wait a couple of years to give him a chance.'

Terri could not believe it. 'You'd do that—for Barry?'

'James has convinced me that this will be the making of him.'

'I'm sure he's right,' said Terri at once.

'And if he does prove a success, it will be all thanks to you.'

She shook her head. 'I don't think so. He'd have done it himself before long, but thank you, Kiel, for giving him this chance.' Impulsively she stood on tiptoe and kissed his cheek, forgetting her hurt a few seconds earlier.

The next instant she was pressed hard against him, his mouth moving over hers. Sparks of fire ignited inside her, desire rose like sap in the spring, and she gave herself up to the rapture of his kiss.

Her heart raced faster than it ever had before, the heat of his body seared through her, and she wanted his kiss to go on for ever. The only sounds were the faint mew of a bird and the whisper of the wind through the tree-tops, but even these faded as her heart beats grew louder.

It was a long, drugging kiss, and when Kiel finally

lifted his head she felt as though a part of her was being torn away. She clung desperately, letting him know that she wanted more, but he determinedly released her. His smile was gentle, though, and she did not feel rejected, simply that it was an interlude before he started again.

He blew hot and cold, this man. Terri never knew in what mood she would find him. But she was grateful for his attention, she had craved it all day, and it had been agony having him so close and yet so distant.

It looked as if he was prepared to be friends again now that Barry was being shunted away. It was not a very satisfactory situation, but the moment was too good to spoil.

'There is one stipulation,' he said, 'about Barry setting up on his own.'

She looked at him. She was floating on cloud nine and almost couldn't care.

He smiled down at her. 'Don't you want to know what it is?'

Terri shrugged. 'Knowing you, there are bound to be stipulations.'

'But this concerns you.'

Her eyes widened. 'Me?'

He nodded. 'I'm lending Barry this money on the understanding that he doesn't have you working for him.'

Terri's blood suddenly ran cold. So they were back to that again! She hadn't been wrong when she guessed Kiel had a reason for bringing her here. It wasn't that she wanted to work for Barry, but Kiel must have thought that if he kissed her, got her fainting in his arms, she wouldn't mind.

But she did—and she eyed him now savagely. 'That's unfair!' she protested.

'It would be unfair on Barry if you worked with him,' he returned calmly. 'He'd never concentrate.'

'And how do you propose keeping us apart?' she demanded, her eyes as dark as a stormy night. 'If Barry wants me I shall go. You won't stop me.'

The thick line of his brows rose. 'Oh, I will, Teresa, make no mistake about that.'

'You sound very sure,' she thrust, her throat arched aggressively.

He smiled grimly. 'I am. With Barry out of the way, there's no reason why you shouldn't work for me. You're very efficient. I'm more than pleased with your performance. I want you to come back—permanently.'

'Do I have a choice?' she asked, feeling breathless all of a sudden. It was what she wanted more than anything in the world—but under these circumstances?

He put his hands on her shoulders and forced her to look into the greyness of his eyes. 'None at all.'

She felt she was drowning in their depths. Her voice was faint. 'You can't make me.'

The next moment his mouth swooped on hers. 'Can't I? Can't I, Teresa?'

In that instant she knew all was lost, knew that with this sort of persuasion there was no way she could refuse. It was emotional blackmail in the extreme.

She had no intention of succumbing easily, though. She struggled to release her mouth, pushing her hands against the solid hardness of his chest. 'Let me go, Kiel! You have no right doing this to me.'

'Don't try saying it's not what you want. Your body gives you away every time. You're a vibrantly responsive woman.'

'And you're taking advantage!'

He smiled. 'It's certainly a pleasant way of persuading you to change your mind.'

E

'You were the one who changed your mind,' she said crossly. 'You sent me away, you backed out of our agreement.'

Kiel shrugged, mouth twisting wryly. 'It was for Barry I did it.'

'Barry can look after himself.'

'Can he?' He looked at her sceptically. 'He's made a mess of his life so far. I'm hoping it will be a thing of the past, but only if you keep out of his way.'

'Are you suggesting that I end our long-standing friendship simply because you don't approve?' He really was expecting a lot!

He gave a snort of impatience. 'I'm not suggesting you end anything, Teresa, just don't go and work for him. Seeing each other occasionally is a different matter.'

'I'm not sure that I want to work for you, now I know the sort of man you are!' she flashed, anger like a tight ball of fire inside her.

Kiel looked surprised. 'I've always considered myself very fair.'

'Then you haven't looked deep into your soul,' she snapped. 'You've hardly treated me fairly.'

'Because,' he said coldly, impatiently, 'Barry hasn't treated *me* fairly. I could have saved you a journey if he'd told me who you were.'

'He probably didn't realise you'd react so violently,' she flashed.

'Oh, I'm quite sure he did.' Kiel nodded slowly to emphasise his words. 'What he didn't count on was my sending you away.'

'You're very hard,' said Terri. 'I'm sure he's not so bad as you make out.'

'Not even after what he did to you?' He looked as though he could scarcely believe her.

She shrugged. 'It won't happen again. We've reached an understanding.'

'An understanding—with Barry?' Kiel's brows rose sceptically. 'He'll say anything to get out of a situation, he's a past master at it, but I would certainly never believe him.'

'Because you're biased,' she snapped. 'You're the most unreasonable man I've ever met!'

'And you now wish you didn't have to come and work for me?' A sudden spark of amusement lightened his eyes.

'Precisely.' Terri glared hostilely. 'In fact, I think I'll stay on here with your parents for a few more days' holiday first.'

His lips firmed and the humour disappeared, but he said, 'Actually, it would be best. Barry won't move out straight away, he has to look for suitable premises. Another stipulation I made was that he's not to set up practice within a thirty-mile radius. I don't want him weaning away my patients.'

'And you're also making sure he'll be too far away for me to bump into accidentally?'

'That's right,' he returned imperturbably.

'I should hate you,' Terri said ruefully.

'But you don't?'

She wondered whether he would be shocked if she told him she loved him. He had figured in her thoughts constantly since that first meeting, and it would break her heart to go away and never see him again.

How would he have reacted, though, had she stuck to her principles and said no? He couldn't have forced her to work for him, no man on earth could make her do anything she did not want to do.

If her feelings for him had not been so strong, she would certainly have told him what to do with his job. In fact, she wondered whether she ought to have done so anyway. What was the point in creating unhappiness, because surely that was what she was doing?

There were no feelings for her on his side. He used her. Every time he wanted something he took advantage of the fact that her resistance was low where he was concerned.

'I'd like to go back now,' she said quietly. And as she had known he would do he turned and began the descent. He had got what he wanted; there was no need to be nice to her any longer.

By the time they reached the cottage Terri had worked herself up into a bitter mood, and as soon as they were indoors she went straight to her room, declining his offer of a drink. Even Pamela, and James, who had returned in their absence, looked surprised when she swept through with a cursory good night.

Why had she done it? she asked herself a thousand times during the next few hours. Why hadn't she been strong and stuck up for herself? Why had she let Kiel have his own way?

The answer was simple. Kiel was the stronger of the two. Kiel *always* got his own way. And didn't she want to work for him? Working with a man she had grown to love must surely be extremely satisfying.

She went to sleep worrying, but awoke feeling surprisingly calm. In fact, the more she thought about it the more she looked forward to the job. It was a challenge. She would prove to Kiel what a good worker she was. She would not let sex enter into it. If he made any advances she would keep him at arm's length.

When she went downstairs her smile was bright. Pamela and Kiel were in the kitchen, James inevitably outside. There was a slightly questioning look on the face Kiel turned towards her, but when he saw her good humour, he too smiled.

'You look much better this morning,' said Pamela, 'and Kiel's just told me the good news.'

Terri knew his mother would be pleased. 'I'm quite looking forward to it,' she said, sliding on to the pine bench beside her hostess.

'And Barry setting up on his own.' Pamela was full of it this morning. 'It's like a dream come true. James is so happy for him. I'm also glad, Terri, that you've decided to stay on here a while longer.'

'If you don't mind?' returned Terri shyly.

'Of course not.' Pamela looked surprised. 'You must visit us as often as you like. It's doubtful we shall see much of the boys, they'll be far too busy.'

'Oh, you never know, Mother,' put in Kiel. 'I might surprise you. I might even come along with Teresa.'

'That would be nice, dear,' said Pamela.

But Terri was not so thrilled. If the truth were known he was afraid to let her out of his sight. He suspected she might shoot across to wherever Barry installed himself. What a nasty, suspicious mind he had!

After breakfast he surprised her by saying, 'I'm taking you out, Teresa. Go and get ready.'

Her brows shot up. 'What if I don't want to go?'

'That's right, you tell him,' said Pamela strongly. 'Kiel always thinks people will fall in with his plans. He's so used to being in command that it never occurs to him that people have minds of their own.'

But to be truthful Terri did not want to refuse. The thought of a whole day in Kiel's company was bliss. His was a suggestion with which she wholeheartedly agreed—even though she made token resistance.

CHAPTER EIGHT

THEY drove to Windermere and joined the crowd on a steamer trip along its length. Kiel indicated various Victorian mansions that had been built for Lancashire mill owners fallen prey to the aesthetic beauty of the lakes.

'Oh, look!' Terri exclaimed suddenly, pointing to an extra large white building with dozens of windows and wide sweeping lawns. 'Who lives there?'

He shrugged. 'I don't know who lives there now, but at one time, long before steamers were a regular part of the scene, a wealthy industrialist owned it. He followed the most amazing ritual every working day of his life.'

'Which was?' urged Terri, her eyes still on the white house.

'It's difficult to believe,' he smiled, 'but each morning he walked down those very lawns to his waiting yacht, preceded, of course, by his butler carrying his breakfast. He would travel up the lake to Lakeside, eating his breakfast on the way, then get into his private coach which took him to Barrow-in-Furness where he worked. At night the procedure was reversed, and he had dinner on his yacht before getting home.'

Terri laughed delightedly. 'How marvellous! I can just imagine him. Don't you think the old days were far grander than they are now?'

'They certainly built some very fine houses,' he agreed. 'Look, there's the Round House.' They were passing Bell Isle, the largest of the group of islands in the centre of the lake. 'Did you know it was the first round house to be built in England?'

Terri shook her head.

'Wordsworth likened it to a pepperpot.'

'I can see why,' she smiled. 'I'm glad you brought me here, Kiel. It's lovely.' She only wished they were alone, that they were not surrounded by throngs of holidaymakers.

Nevertheless it did not detract from the dramatic scenery, the fells rising steeply from the sides of the silver water, the Gothic follies that appeared and disappeared. Scores of tiny boats littered the surface. It was a busy, happy scene, and she was glad to be a part of it.

After their steamer trip they went to Troutbeck. 'The most picturesque village in Lakeland,' Kiel informed her proudly.

They went inside Town End, a National Trust property still occupied by descendants of the family who had built it back in the days of Henry VIII. In one of its rooms was a most beautiful fourposter bed, and at the foot a fourposter cradle. Terri was enchanted.

And all the while they were doing this, all the time they were exploring, Kiel was at his most attentive. He treated her as though she were a precious possession, attuned to her every need, his hand on her elbow as they moved through the jostling crowds.

Terri could not help responding, and found it difficult to believe she had known Kiel for such a short length of time. In the mood he was in they were completely compatible. She felt very special, and wanted this day to go on for ever.

'Where now?' he asked.

'Hill Top Farm,' she said at once.

'I didn't know you were a Beatrix Potter fan?' he smiled.

She nodded enthusiastically. 'I loved Peter Rabbit when I was a child, and I've often wondered what sort of a person she was.'

And so they went to Sawrey and visited the farm, which also belonged to the National Trust. Terri wandered through the rooms of the grey stone building, imagining Beatrix Potter sitting here writing her stories about Jemima Puddleduck, Mrs Tiggy-Winkle and all the rest of them.

She was disappointed when Kiel announced it was time to go home. But she certainly could not complain about her day. She felt wonderfully, gloriously happy. He had shown her no more than ordinary common courtesy, yet she read into it something more and felt as high as a kite.

Pamela had their evening meal ready and was eager to hear about their day, listening attentively to Terri's description of Hill Top Farm.

Afterwards Terri asked whether she might phone Richard. 'He'll be so surprised to hear I'm staying after all. He'll wonder what's going on.'

He was indeed astonished, but happy for her too, and especially elated when she told him about Barry.

Making her way back to the sitting-room Terri heard Kiel say firmly, 'It's not something I wanted to do, you understand, but what I had to do. You need a good atmosphere when you're working with someone. There's no point in being at daggers drawn.'

Terri felt a chill steal over her. So taking her out had been a conditioning process, nothing more. What a good actor he was, how completely he had fooled her!

By the end of the day she had been his to do with as he liked. He must have sensed this, yet hadn't taken advantage. Now she knew why.

It took every ounce of willpower to go into the room and pretend there was nothing wrong. It was such an ordeal that she excused herself early on the pretext that her day out had made her tired.

If she had any sense she would go home, leave the Lakes for good. But Kiel's magnetism was too strong and she knew she would stay for as long as there was a job, even though the pain might at times be unbearable.

The next morning she discovered that Kiel had been called away early on an urgent case and would not be back. He had done what he'd set out to do, she thought bitterly, there was no need for him to stay any longer.

At least it would give her a breathing space, time to adjust to the fact that she would never mean anything to Kiel. Yet the more she thought about him the more deeply she realised she loved him. It was a futile love, she knew, but there was nothing she could do about it. When a person fell in love it wasn't to order, it just happened. And it had happened to her, when she was least expecting it, and to a man who did not want it.

The days passed pleasantly enough, strolling into the village, helping Pamela with the housework, telling James how lovely his roses were.

It was after supper more than a week later when Pamela announced that Kiel was on the telephone for her. Terri's heart pounded irrationally as she picked up the receiver.

'Barry's gone,' he said without preamble. 'I'd like you here first thing in the morning.'

He didn't waste words, thought Terri miserably.

There was no soft talk now. He was ready for her and she had to jump.

'I'll be there,' she said, and the line went dead. She turned to Pamela who was hovering behind her. 'Kiel wants me at the surgery tomorrow. I'm afraid my holiday is over.'

The older woman nodded. 'I believe Barry's been lucky and dropped on the practice of a retiring doctor somewhere just north of Carlisle. He's decided to go and familiarise himself with things while the other man's still around.'

Terri nodded. 'Kiel did say he'd left.'

Pamela looked at her sharply. 'You sound bitter?'

'I'd have liked to see Barry again, that's all.' Terri dared not tell the woman the real reason.

'He's not gone to the ends of the earth,' smiled Mrs Allen. 'But I'm sure it's not only that. You've been very preoccupied lately. Is something wrong? Can you tell me about it?'

Terri shook her head. If she confessed to overhearing Kiel's confidence, Pamela would naturally stick up for her son. It was something she had to live with. 'I'm a little apprehensive, that's all; afraid of letting Kiel down.'

'Heavens, you needn't worry on that score,' said Pamela. 'Kiel's very impressed with the way you work. He said you knock some other nurses into fits.'

Terri smiled wanly. 'A few days, that's all I did.'

'Time enough,' said the older woman. 'Kiel's a very good judge and he wouldn't suggest you work for him if he didn't think you were good enough.'

'Then I'm worrying for nothing.' Terri gave what she hoped was a convincing smile.

When she got to the surgery the next morning, however, she knew her fears were founded. Kiel treated her with a brusqueness that was at complete odds with the act he had put on the last time she had seen him.

They were busy, she had to admit, the surgery going on for much longer than usual due to Barry's absence. He went out on his calls afterwards, but no sooner had she cleaned up and sorted herself out than it was time for the evening session.

She was glad when it was all over, relieved too that all she had to do was go upstairs to the flat. She ate a leisurely meal, took a shower, and went to bed.

She was woken by the sound of breaking glass downstairs. The hairs on the back of her neck prickled and she broke out into a cold sweat. Someone had forced their way in! Ought she to investigate, or was that foolhardy? She might get herself killed. Perhaps it was best to phone the police.

Terri climbed out of bed, careful to make no noise, glancing out of the window as she made her way through to the sitting-room. If there was a get-away vehicle the police would want a description.

And there it was. A white car. *Kiel's car!* It was Kiel! What was he doing here? Was there some emergency?

She dragged on her housecoat and rushed down to the surgery. Kiel was bent over a broken bottle, sweeping up the fragments. He looked at her impatiently when she entered. 'What the hell do you want?'

For once his aggressive tones did not bother her. She was too busy staring at him. There was blood on his hands, on his clothes, everywhere—and not from the glass. Oil smeared his face and the sleeves of his shirt, and he looked so tired her heart bled for him.

'What have you been doing?' she gasped.

He stood up, hands on hips, stretching his back. 'A road accident. I've been there for hours. They had to cut the driver out. He's lucky to be alive. It's certainly one holiday he'll never forget!'

'You should have phoned me,' said Terri at once. 'Maybe I could have helped.'

Kiel shook his head. 'The ambulance was there. Those guys know what they're doing. But I must re-stock my bag. You never know, I might get called out again.'

She hoped not, he needed some sleep. He looked as though he'd had none for a week.

'Why don't you come up to the flat and have a shower?' she suggested, when he'd put all the necessary supplies into his bag. 'I'll make you some coffee.'

He nodded. 'Mm, I'd like that.'

He almost fell asleep over his drink. Knowing she risked his wrath, Terri ventured tentatively, 'If you like, you can sleep in Barry's old room. You don't look as though you have the energy to drive home.'

'It's been a hell of a day,' he admitted, 'but there's something I could do with more than sleep.' His eyes rested somnolently on her, drooping lids hiding his expression. 'Come here, Teresa.'

His voice was low and sensual and sent tiny shivers down her spine. More than anything she wanted to go to him, but she deliberately hesitated, fearing reprisal. You never knew with Kiel what would happen next. 'That's not what I'm offering,' she muttered.

'I know,' he said, 'but surely you're not going to refuse me?' He pulled himself up out of the chair, his eyes not once leaving her face, moving with agonising slowness towards her.

He had changed into a shirt and pants that he kept here for emergencies such as this, and he smelled clean and vibrantly masculine. When his mouth claimed hers in a long drugging kiss Terri's response was automatic. No matter what she thought, her need was deep.

Nor could she stop him when he stripped off her housecoat and slid her nightdress down over her shoulders.

His hands slid exploratively over her scented skin, causing her responsive breasts to harden, pulling her hard against him. 'I've wanted to do this ever since you came through the surgery door looking like an angel of mercy,' he groaned.

Terri said nothing, enjoying the moment while it lasted, involuntarily arching herself against him.

His lips burned a trail down the column of her throat and when he took each proud nipple in turn into his mouth, she felt as though she was ready to explode.

'Teresa, I want you,' he mouthed hoarsely.

She merely moaned in response, wanting him too, achingly, desperately. He slid one hand beneath her knees, the other behind her shoulders, and lifting her carried her towards the bedroom.

It was then that Terri came to her senses. Letting Kiel have his way with her now would only cause more heartache later, give him further reason to despise her.

'No, Kiel! No!' She pummelled her fists into his chest.

His head jerked. 'Why? Because it's me and not Barry? You invited me up here, don't forget.'

'But not for this,' she cried. 'I felt sorry for you because you looked tired, I didn't expect you to take advantage.' Why was she saying this when her whole body craved him? Why was she denying herself the pleasure he would undoubtedly give?

'Teresa, you want me as much as I want you. It's

been that way ever since we first met. Can you deny it?'

Dumbly she shook her head.

'But there's Barry to consider, isn't there?' His tone was barely civil. 'But Barry's not here, and I am—and I want you.'

As she wanted him. He laid her down on the bed and began ripping off his own clothes. First his shirt, revealing his tanned muscled chest with its scattering of fair hairs.

'Please, Kiel,' Terri implored.

'Please what?' he sneered.

'Please don't do this to me.'

'You don't sound very convincing. Are you sure it's not just the proprieties you're worried about? No one will ever know.'

'I couldn't give a damn what people think,' she snapped. 'You once said you never force yourself upon a woman.' Her mouth was desperately dry.

'I don't intend forcing myself on you, Teresa. Tell me you don't want me to touch you. Tell me you don't want my kisses. Go on, damn you, tell me!'

How could she when her whole body ached for him, when there was a desperate kind of longing inside her which only he could fulfil? But she knew that his only reason was because he needed a woman, any woman would do. It just so happened that she was handy.

Her voice was a mere whisper as she spoke. 'I don't want you to touch me. Either go into the other room and let me sleep or, if that's too much for you, get out altogether. Go home. I don't want you to make love to me.'

His eyes hardened and he frowned. 'You sound as though you mean it?'

'I do,' she said. 'I've never been more sincere in my life.'

Kiel swung away savagely. 'If I weren't so damn tired I'd be tempted to persuade you to change your mind. As it is . . .' He passed a hand wearily over his brow. 'You can consider yourself safe. I haven't the strength to fight you, not tonight. But I haven't given up.'

Terri shook her head. 'Why, Kiel? Why are you doing this to me?' He was making it so hard for her.

'I wish I knew,' he said tiredly, then swung round and was gone. Terri felt a pang of regret, but it was momentary. Kiel was simply trying to keep things sweet between them. He didn't want to work with someone at daggers drawn, he had said.

Two hours later Terri was still wide awake, too conscious of Kiel being next door to relax. She called herself all sorts of a fool for stopping him when in reality she wanted him to make love to her. It had been wrong to suggest he stay here. She would certainly never make the same mistake again.

At six she heard him up and about and guessed that he too had had difficulty in sleeping, but when her door opened some minutes later he looked as fresh and vital as if he had slept for eight hours.

'I couldn't find anything in your store cupboard for breakfast,' he said apologetically. 'But I've made some tea and toast, if that will do.'

It was so unexpected she beamed. 'Lovely!'

She sat up and settled the tray on her knees. There was something comforting about being looked after by this man, and she did not feel at all shy that he was in her bedroom.

'When you've finished,' he said, 'go back to sleep for an hour. I'm going home to get changed.'

'I am tired,' she admitted, wondering why he was being so considerate all of a sudden. 'I couldn't sleep.'

'I know,' he smiled. 'I heard you tossing and turning.'

So he hadn't slept either! It was small consolation.

When he had gone the flat felt empty. Disturbing though Kiel's presence was, she missed him. But replete with the toast and tea she curled between the sheets and in seconds was asleep.

Again she was disturbed, this time by the telephone. Groaning inwardly, Terri dragged herself out of bed. It surely wasn't Kiel again?

'Terri, is that you?'

The voice was familiar yet it took a moment or two to recognise it. 'Michael?'

'The very same.'

Her heart did a downward plummet. How had he traced her here? Didn't he realise that the fact she had left London without leaving him a message meant she wanted nothing more to do with him? But Michael had always been persistent. He never took no for an answer.

'How are you?' she ventured. 'How did the trip go?'

'Who cares about Venezuela?' he boomed. 'I want to know what you're doing up there. Why did you go without telling me? What's it all about?'

He didn't sound very happy, and nor was Terri. 'Did you have to ring so early?' she demanded irritably. 'You've got me out of bed.' It occurred to her that had it been Kiel she would not have been annoyed. Her pulse would have been racing by now, her heartbeats quickened, instead of this heavy sense of foreboding.

'I didn't want to disturb you while you were working,' he said.

'You could have rung tonight.' Or you needn't have bothered at all, she added silently. She had never encouraged Michael, always told him she did not love him. But he wouldn't give up. She guessed he never would until she was out of his reach by being married to someone else.

'And risk you being out? No, thanks, Terri, my darling. It was bad enough getting back and finding you gone. I went straight round to see you. You could have knocked me down with a feather when Richard told me what had happened!'

'I'm sorry,' she said quietly, cursing her brother for revealing her whereabouts. She would get no peace now, that was for certain. 'I had a chance of this job and I took it. It was unfortunate you were away and I couldn't tell you.' Or providential. Michael would have done his best to talk her out of it. He would never move away from London. He loved the fast pace, the theatre and the parties, the fact that there was always something to do, somewhere to go. He would be bored here in two days flat.

'You didn't go to—get away from me?' The slight pause gave away his uncertainty.

'Of course not,' she said quickly, then realised that she had missed an opportunity to get him off her back. 'With Richard and Rachel taking over the house I'd got to move anyway. It seemed as good a time as any for a complete change of scenery.

'There's always a bed at my place,' he told her.

She knew that. She had lost count of the number of times he had asked her to move in with him. She wondered if he would ever accept no for an answer. 'It's not what I want, you know that. I love it here, Michael. It's different. It's so peaceful and quiet—and beautiful. It must be the prettiest place in the world.'

He snorted angrily. 'Hell, you're too young to bury yourself in the country. What are you thinking of, Terri? Is there some man involved?'

If he could have seen her face he would have known.

She closed her eyes, leaning back against the wall, shaking her head. 'No, no man, Michael.' At least no man who was interested in her.

This was one emotion she and Michael shared. To love someone and not receive their love in return was, she had discovered, the most painful experience in the world. She could sympathise with him, but not help.

She heard his sigh of relief. 'Then I suppose I must wait for you to get fed up with the quiet life and come home. You will come back, Terri?'

'I expect so, one day,' she said quietly, but without enthusiasm. It all depended on Kiel. Such were his irrational changes of mood that he could kick her out without warning.

'And you will keep in touch?'

'I'll keep in touch.'

'And you'll let me know if there's anyone else so that I can come and punch his face in?'

A laugh accompanied his words, but Terri knew he was deadly serious. 'You won't have to do that, Michael. I'm enjoying my job too much to bother with men. But please don't wait for me. I've told you how I feel and I haven't changed. I don't love you. You're wasting your life. Find someone else to love. Please!'

There was silence for a moment, then he said faintly, 'You're asking the impossible.'

Perhaps she was, but he had to accept the fact that she would never marry him. When he eventually said goodbye, Terri was left with the feeling that he was one hell of an unhappy man. She felt guilty, but what could she do? She had never given Michael any encouragement. He knew exactly how she felt. Perhaps with her out of the way he would find another girl. She hoped so, she really did.

She stepped beneath the shower and by the time she

had finished all thoughts of Michael had fled, Kiel alone occupied her mind.

She loved him more deeply than she had ever imagined. Michael's telephone call had forcibly brought home the fact. Yet it was a pointless love. Kiel would never return it. He still thought she had come here after Barry. He thought she was the type to throw herself at any man. Hadn't she virtually done it to him?

Did Michael feel as hopeless as she did? It had never occurred to her before how it must hurt. Now he probably felt even worse. But perhaps he was finally convinced? With a bit of luck he would forget her.

But how could you forget a person you loved? She would never forget Kiel. Even if she left here today the memory of him would be with her for all time.

Eagerly now, she got dressed. In another few minutes he would be here. Another day in close contact. Each one more precious than the last. She had to take advantage of every moment spent with him because she never knew when it would all end.

By the time the last patient of the evening had gone, she felt exhausted. Kiel looked tired too, making his suggestion all the more surprising. 'How would you like to come out to dinner with me?'

How would she like it? It was with greatest difficulty that she stopped herself from jumping for joy, and her answer was so long in coming that he continued, 'If you're too tired, just say the word.'

Terri quickly nodded. 'I would like to come. Just name the time and I'll be ready. What do I wear, something dressy or casual?'

The look he gave her was long and assessing, causing her adrenalin to flow. 'You always look good, you must know that. I'll leave it to you, whatever you wear will be right.'

A warmth stole over her and she turned away so that he should not see the sudden rush of colour to her cheeks. She was not sure whether he was complimenting her or not. She felt pleased, but it was stupid to read too much into his casual words.

'I'll pick you up at eight, that gives you an hour. Think you can make it?'

She nodded, wondering what sort of girls he dated if they took any longer. She could do it in five minutes if necessary.

'You've gone very quiet.' His voice was close in her ear.

Terri felt the burning warmth of his body and turned, then wished she hadn't when she found his mouth inches away from her own. She could not take her eyes from the sensual fulness and unconsciously ran the tip of her tongue across her own suddenly dry lips.

She had the feeling he was offering her more than a meal, and her whole body cried out in response to the doctor who had turned without warning into an exciting male animal.

With an effort she lifted her eyes to his, drawing in a tight breath at his flare of desire, then letting out a soft moan as he gathered her into his arms.

CHAPTER NINE

KIEL'S kiss was disappointingly short. It seemed that no sooner had he claimed Terri's lips than he let her go. She felt an overwhelming urge to cling, to beg for more, to offer herself to him.

But that was probably what he expected. He must have felt her immediate response, the eagerness with which she accepted. Could that be why he had called an immediate halt? Had she been too ready to show him that she was willing? Shame now coloured her cheeks. She had quite possibly ruined what could have been a wonderful evening.

'I'd better go,' he said, 'or we might not manage that meal at all.' His voice was thick with raw emotion and when she dared glance at him she saw that he was as disturbed by the fleeting kiss as herself. He was not disgusted, or triumphant, or any of the other feelings she expected.

Elation returned, and her face split with a Cheshire Cat grin. 'I won't keep you waiting.'

She was upstairs and in her flat almost before he started his engine. Then came the problem of what to wear. Not the pink silk, it was far too formal, and the white cotton too girlish. She wanted something to fit her mood. She felt on top of the world, happy, sexy, and bubbling with life.

She plucked an electric-blue dress from the back of her wardrobe. It was short, figure-moulding and daring. She had worn it only once and it had excited so many comments that she had never dared wear it again. But she wanted Kiel to notice her, to desire her, and this was the very thing.

She showered hastily, shampooed her hair and blow dried it into soft bouncy waves, leaving it thick and loose to fall provocatively about her face.

Make-up she kept to a minimum, a dab of powder, eyeshadow to match the dress, mascara to darken and thicken her lashes, and a touch of lip gloss. A spray of a wickedly expensive perfume, turquoise droppers in her ears, a quick shrug into the dress, and she was ready.

Her reflection in the somewhat ancient mirror was more than satisfactory. Excitement had added colour to her cheeks and she looked how she felt—full of anticipation for a date with the man she loved.

The moment she heard his car she wanted to run down the steps and meet him, but prudence told her to sit demurely and wait. She had the door open, though, when he reached it and the look of admiration in his eyes gave her the answer she wanted.

The dress plunged to a vee at both back and front, exposing enough cleavage to be tantalising without being vulgar. It clipped her waist, smoothed her hips, and revealed a long length of bare leg. Silver strappy sandals completed the outfit.

'You approve?' she asked coquettishly, giving him a twirl and then coming to a halt daringly close, an impish smile curving her lips, her violet eyes alight with good humour.

'Very much so. I think I've changed my mind abut going out. I'm almost afraid to let anyone else see you. You're ravishing, do you know that?'

'You're a flatterer.' Her heart beat erratically, her breathing became shallow and uneven. 'And I'm starving. You're not backing out on your offer of a meal?' She had never before felt so at ease with Kiel.

For once they were on equal terms—and she liked it. Very much.

'I'm hungry too, more's the pity,' he said. And as if with an effort turned and led the way from the room.

Terri followed closely, sliding into his car as he held open the door, feeling the tingling torment of his eyes as they slid over her thighs when her dress rode high.

His car seemed smaller, more intimate, thrusting her so close she could feel his warmth, inhale his strong masculine smell, almost taste the sexual vitality of him.

He made sure she was comfortable before setting off, leaning across to check her seatbelt, the brush of his arm against her breast sending sweet exquisite frissons of delight through her nerve-stream.

With one last smouldering look he set the car in motion. Terri's stomach churned with a mixture of feelings and she was afraid to look at him. But she could not concentrate on the road ahead, or the beautiful Lakeland scenery, and without conscious thought turned her head in his direction.

He wore a pair of pale slacks and a dark velvet jacket, each moulding itself to the hard contours of his body. A crisp white shirt complemented his healthy tan, a silk tie perfectly matching the colour of his trousers.

His hand left the wheel to rest briefly on her leg, the feel of his lean fingers remaining long after his hand had gone. Her inner agony increased and she wanted to touch him in return but was afraid.

She had to be careful that he did not get the wrong impression. She did not want him to retain the idea that she was free with her emotions. No man had ever, ever, exhorted from her such intense feelings of longing and desire. It was a new experience.

During the short drive to the restaurant he

remained silent and she was glad. She wanted nothing to break these moments of quiet intimacy. He might not be feeling as deeply emotional, but for once he was not being antagonistic. He seemed to be actually enjoying her company, wanting it, and she found the moments too precious to spoil by pointless conversation.

He had already made the reservation and was welcomed warmly by the manager, who appeared to know him well.

They sat in the embrace of a round bow window and Kiel ordered their drinks. The countryside unfolded before them like a picture postcard. High fells and lush meadows, a sparkling stream and graceful trees. Outside was an oasis of peace, in her heart a storm raged.

She wondered how she was going to get through the whole evening without giving away the intense feelings effervescing inside her. They were clamouring for escape, wanting to let this man know exactly how she felt.

'Are you missing Barry?'

The question took her by surprise, causing her head to jerk back, her eyes to widen, and a tiny portion of her pleasure disappeared. She didn't want to discuss Barry. 'Not really, why?'

His broad shoulders lifted easily. 'He was the main reason you were here.'

'No, he wasn't.' Terri determined to keep her voice even, not to let him see that he could ruin what had promised to be a special evening. 'I really have no feelings at all where Barry is concerned, not in the way you're suggesting.'

'It wouldn't matter to you if you never saw him again?'

Their eyes met and held as though locked together

and it was a minute before Terri could reply. She was fascinated by the steely grey depths, the black line surrounding the iris that looked as if it had been painted with a fine brush, emphasising them, giving them a startling clarity. She felt sure he could see into her soul. That he knew the answer to every question before she gave it.

'Not really,' she managed at length, 'although he has been a friend for a long time. Months and months sometimes go by without me or Richard seeing him, then he'll turn up——'

'Like the proverbial bad penny?'

She ignored his jibe. 'And we'll both be glad to see him.'

Their drinks came and she sipped her Martini gratefully, glad of something to take her attention off Kiel.

'So you're not—and never have been—lovers?'

'Most definitely not!' she flared, then realising she had raised her voice, even though she intended remaining calm, said more quietly, 'You insult me by even suggesting it.'

He looked slightly shamefaced. 'I didn't mean to, but it is—important to me. The night that Barry—assaulted you, was that the first time he'd ever touched you?'

Terri's heart turned over and she looked away, unprepared when his hard fingers touched her chin, compelling her to face him again. There was pain in her eyes and he frowned, his brows jagged.

'It's not the first time he's forced himself on you?'

She didn't want to tell him, but numbly she nodded, the admission dragged from her as surely as if he had fed her a truth drug.

Terri heard the whistling noise as he drew in a swift breath. 'When?'

She swallowed convulsively and closed her eyes. 'I was just sixteen. He said I was—old enough—and that I ought to—find out what life had to offer. That he would teach me.'

'God, if I'd known!' Kiel's voice grated harshly in the silence of the room and Terri was glad there was no one present to observe her torment. 'I'd never have thrust you together. I played right into his hands. Can you ever forgive me?'

'It was a thing of the past,' said Terri quickly. 'I'd forgotten it. I never thought he'd try it again. I thought I'd convinced him that I didn't want that sort of relationship.'

'He must have known, when he told your brother about the vacancy, that you'd apply. Barry can be very devious when it comes to getting his own way. He was simply biding his time before trying again. You'd be a challenge to him, Teresa. It's a rare girl turns him down.'

Terri's mouth was dry and she took a long swallow of Martini. 'If he touches me again, I'll be sick. I can stand him as a friend, but that's all.'

'I believe you,' he said. 'I guess I should have believed you all along. You're not Barry's type at all, I can see that now.' His grey eyes grew warm and he rested his hand on top of hers.

A tremor ran through Terri and at that moment the waiter brought their menus. She did not know whether to be glad or sorry that the moment had been spoilt. What she needed to know was whether she was Kiel's type? That was the important question and she might have found out had they not been interrupted.

She glanced at the menu, not really caring what she ate, in the end leaving the choice to Kiel, hoping that if they made their decision quickly they might return to the conversation.

But instead, Kiel began to talk about the accident last night, and several others that had occurred in recent months, and she guessed the opportunity was lost for ever.

Soon they were shown to their table in an intimate corner of the restaurant. The several other couples present were oblivious to anyone else. It ws evidently a place for lovers, thought Terri, and wondered why Kiel had brought her here.

Her glance flicked around the room and back to him, and he knew what she was thinking. 'A nice place, don't you agree?' he asked with a smile. If you don't want to be disturbed.'

And was that why he had brought her here? It was like a dream come true and she mentally crossed her fingers that he would not be called out. There was no Barry to help now. He had to deal with any emergencies himself.

The devilled mushrooms in garlic sauce were delicious. Terri ate hungrily. 'I'm glad I didn't have to go back to London,' she said.

He eyed her steadily. 'If you'd said that to me a few days ago I'd have thought it was because of Barry. Tell me, exactly why were you running away?'

Terri frowned. 'From home? I told you, Richard got married and the house is now his. I've not seen much of England, so it seemed the ideal time for a change.'

'But why here exactly? The Lakes are no place for a nubile girl. Or is it your intention never to get married? Have you a down on men for some reason? Or——' He paused, eyeing her speculatively. Terri felt an odd shiver run through her. 'Is there some man behind it all? There has to be a logical reason, and I don't buy the tale that it was because you'd sold your brother your half of the house.'

If Michael had not phoned Terri would have denied the point emphatically, but coming so close after his call she found herself hesitating, avoiding Kiel's eyes, looking anywhere but at him.

'I'm waiting,' he urged softly.

From beneath lowered lids she looked at him. His eyes were intent upon her face, piercing, probing, missing nothing. But Michael was of secondary importance, and in all honesty she had not been running away from him. He had been out of the country when she left.

'There's no one,' she said quietly, steadily. 'No one at all.' Michael knew exactly where he stood with her. There should be no further calls from him now.

She held his gaze, not realising she was holding her breath as well. He seemed to be deliberating whether to accept that she was speaking the truth.

After what seemed an eternity he visibly relaxed. 'That's good.' His voice was a low soft growl.

She let out her own breath. They had both been as taut as violin strings. Now he smiled and reached for her hand across the table. A searing warmth raced through Terri, her eyes locked into his, and she felt that at last she was getting somewhere.

Their main course arrived, but Terri found it difficult to eat. Hunger of a different kind filled her. Hunger for this man, who had just given the impression that he was interested. He had accepted that Barry meant nothing, that there was no one else, and she felt sure he now meant to stake a claim.

But even if that was the case it did not put him off his food. Unlike herself, he cleared his plate. Although the veal escalopes were tender and tasty Terri could not finish them.

'What's happened to your appetite?' Kiel watched

with a faint frown as she pushed the food about her plate.

Terri could not believe he did not know, he was usually so good at reading her mind. Unless she had misinterpreted the signs? Her violet eyes widened as she looked across the table. 'It's very filling.'

'And you're a liar.' The words were accompanied by a smile, a smile that softened his features, gentled his eyes. 'But I shall not force you to eat, not on this occasion. You do realise, though, the importance of eating properly?'

'Yes, doctor,' she husked with pretended innocence.

'The last thing I want is a nurse faint from lack of proper nourishment.'

'I promise not to faint on you.' She could not take her eyes away from his face. The eternal magnet drew her to him and she wanted this moment to go on for ever. It was the first time she had ever felt so close, felt that there was a reasonable chance of him returning her feelings.

He refilled her wine glass and, the tension broken, Terri managed another mouthful of food. But her heart pounded like a sledgehammer and all she wanted was to go home. She wanted Kiel to accompany her to the flat and take her into his arms and kiss her again. A long satisfying kiss, not a mere taste of what he had to offer.

She needed satisfaction, not a hungering for more. Surely he knew that? Surely he knew how she felt? The waiter removed their plates. She declined a sweet and Kiel ordered coffee.

She drank it strong and black and he suggested they leave the moment they had finished. Silence had settled between them and she wondered whether he was as anxious as she to be alone. Completely alone! This was a pleasant intimate restaurant, but even so, it was no place to bare your soul.

By the time they got back to the flat, Terri had worked herself up into such a state that it was a real effort to refrain from throwing herself at Kiel.

He did not wait for her to invite him in, following her up the steps, confident in the knowledge that this was what she wanted.

Her face was glowing, her eyes very bright, when the door closed behind them. She turned to face him and he held out his arms—and the telephone rang. She could have screamed.

At first she ignored it, moving reluctantly only when Kiel said, 'I think you'd better answer it.' She hoped it wasn't Michael again.

'Hi, Terri!' Barry's cheerful voice came over the line. 'How're you doing?'

Her spirits dropped. Barry was almost as bad. What did he want, for heaven's sake? Couldn't he have timed it better? 'Okay, and you? Are you settling in?'

'Not too bad, you know. How's Kiel treating you? Better now, I hope?'

'Actually he's here,' said Terri, turning to find Kiel's frowning gaze upon her. She silently cursed Barry for his inopportune call.

'So what are you two up to?' Barry's deep chuckle reverberated in her ear. 'As a matter of fact it's Kiel I want. Mrs Barnes said I might find him there. Terri, I——'

But Terri was not listening. She held out the phone. 'It's for you.'

Black brows rose. 'Barry?'

She nodded, careful not to let his hand touch hers as he took the instrument, moving across the room and looking out of the window. Kiel's car stood below and she rested her eyes on it, not listening to his conversation, conscious only that Barry had ruined everything.

Kiel would not accept that Barry wanted to speak to him. He would think it an excuse because he had caught them together. He was probably wondering even now how many times his stepbrother had telephoned since he'd moved. He would never believe this was the first.

So deep was she in her misery that she never heard Kiel put down the phone. When his hand touched her shoulder she jumped violently. 'I have to go out,' he said softly. 'I'm sorry, Teresa. I was looking forward to spending some more time with you. It will be late when I get back, I'm afraid. I'll see you in the morning.'

He dropped a gentle kiss to her brow, turned, and was gone. Terri was left feeling dazed. She had expected anger and there was none. Miraculously he had not misconstrued Barry's reason for telephoning. There would be other opportunities, other occasions. The future was suddenly bright again.

Most evenings after that he either joined her at the flat or she went to his house and tucked in to Mrs Barnes' superb cooking. His lovemaking was exciting, but restrained, as though he was still not sure about her. If only she had the courage to tell him exactly how she felt.

But she had no idea what his feelings were. He gave the impression that she was someone special, but she could not be sure. He never said, he never spoke about the future, their future. For all she knew he could simply be amusing himself at her expense.

It was a disquieting thought, but for the present it did not matter. She was content in his company, in the knowledge that he found her attractive and desirable.

After Saturday morning surgery, a couple of weeks later, he made her doubly happy. 'I'm going to visit my parents. Would you like to come?'

Would she? He must have known what her answer would be. And surely this meant he was after more than an affair? Her joy knew no bounds.

'You've settled in much better than I expected,' he said when they began their journey, 'for someone who's lived all her life in the city. You've no regrets?'

Terri smiled. 'None at all.' Although she would not have liked to answer the same question had their relationship been different. Without Kiel her spare time would have dragged. She could have gone for walks, or a drive, but it wouldn't have been the same.

She could see now why he had suspected her reasons for coming here. It was certainly not the sort of place where one could be alone and enjoy it, not at her age anyway.

'Could you spend the rest of your life here, or do you intend returning to London some day?' He did not look at her as he spoke, concentrating on the stretch of road winding along the valley bottom.

The question was casual, but Terri knew he attached importance to her answer. Or was it that she *hoped* he did? She was still not sure exactly where she stood with him.

'If there was reason for me to stay I would,' she answered carefully. 'I think it must be the most beautiful part of England.' Wherever one looked there was natural beauty. Right at this moment, becks splashed down over tumbled boulders, crags peeped out of wooded slopes, ancient cottages were tucked away into folds in the fellsides. Nothing could be more rural, or peaceful—or romantic!'

'What sort of reason?' Kiel still kept his eyes straight in front, giving her no clue at all as to his feelings, or why he was posing these questions. 'Your job? A husband? Or what?'

'Either of those,' she shrugged, attempting to make

her voice light, but afraid she was failing dismally. 'Aren't they the usual reasons that keep a person in one place?'

He was silent for so long that she risked a glance. There was a curve to his lips and he caught her eye for a second. 'I'm debating, on which one I'd like to be your reason for staying. Your job is safe, I can assure you of that. So long as I'm here anyway.'

Terri's head jerked, her heart gave a sudden lurch. 'You're not planning on moving?' The thought dismayed her more than she thought possible. To live here without Kiel would be impossible. She definitely would return to London under those circumstances.

'Not yet,' he returned calmly, 'but as you know, I have other interests.'

Terri nodded. 'If you concentrate solely on nutrition, would you move to one of the major cities?'

'I might have to divide my time, but my real home will always be the Lakes. It's my first love.'

She wondered whether it was insane to be jealous of a slice of the English countryside. She wanted to be his first love, his only love. What could she do to make him love her as she loved him? 'I see.' Her voice echoed her unhappiness.

'You sound as thought you don't like the thought of me leaving?'

She looked down at her hands. 'I don't.'

'Why's that? Are you afraid you might not get on with my successor? I'm sure that won't be the case. You're very good, as you must know.'

Terri's heart dipped lower and lower. All this could mean only one thing—that whatever relationship they shared at the moment, it was not long lasting.

Suddenly Kiel stopped the car, turning in his seat to look at her. 'Teresa, you're upset.' He took her hands and she had no choice but to look at him.

F

Her eyes were wide amethyst orbs, made even larger by the moisture of unshed tears. There was tenderness in his expression such as she had never seen before.

'Why?' The gruff husky whisper was unlike his usual commanding tone.

'Because——' She shrugged. 'Because—I like working with you. It wouldn't be the same with someone else.'

'I'd like to think it's me personally you'd miss?' There was a stillness about him all of a sudden, his eyes intent upon her face.

Terri had difficulty in breathing. He was trying to force an admission that she was not sure she could give—not without knowing how he felt.

'I shall,' she whispered at length, 'very much.'

'Enough to come with me—wherever I go?'

Numbly she nodded. She had no idea what he was getting at, whether it was still a job he was offering, or more? But whatever, just to be with him would be sufficient.

He groaned and the next instant his arms were about her, crushing her to him, his mouth seeking hers, forcing her lips apart to deepen his kiss.

Terri's head began to spin and quite without realising it her arms crept around his neck, her whole body pulsingly and vibratingly alive, returning his kisses with an abandon that she had been scared to show before.

Desire rose and threatened to choke her if she did not find relief. 'Oh, Kiel!' The words were dragged out as he turned his attention to the delicate skin behind her ears, his tongue and lips creating their own erotic sensations. 'Kiel, what are you doing to me?'

It was a cry from the heart and he held her closer. 'The same as you do to me, my love.'

She drew in a deep desperately needed breath and tightened her arms about him. It all sounded too good to be true. It was what she had wanted but never dreamed would happen.

But—did it mean he loved her, or merely found her more desirable? There was a difference, one that could lift her to the heights or send her plummeting down to hell.

His mouth burned a searing trail along the line of her jaw, down the slender column of her arched throat, tasting her, desiring her, increasing her already heightened emotions.

'Teresa, I've fought against you, all my instincts told me it was wrong. Your response when I thought you were Barry's, made me think you were like it with any man. Now I know I was mistaken, that you're nothing like the girl I imagined you to be. Can you forgive me for treating you so shabbily?'

He was actually trembling as he held her in his arms, his face buried against her neck. 'There's nothing to forgive so far as I'm concerned.' Terri raked her fingers through the tousled tawny hair. It was as strong as Kiel himself. She moulded his head between her palms, feeling his shape and warmth. 'You're entitled to your opinions.'

When he looked at her she studied every tiny detail of his face, from the thick brows, the troubled grey eyes, the straight nose, to the full sensual lips which were slightly parted. His breathing was as erratic as her own, a muscle jerking spasmodically in his jaw, a dampness to his brow.

'I don't deserve your generosity.' His voice was no more than a husky whisper, hands heavy on her shoulders, the pressure of his fingertips such that she felt sure he was branding her.

She shook her head gently. 'I'm not generous, I'm

just overwhelmed.' Her eyes were harnessed to his and she could see the pain behind them, the slight narrowing as though he still could not believe what was happening. 'I never thought you'd change, Kiel. I—I've wanted you so much. I've never felt about anyone else like I do about you. Do you really believe in me now, or am I dreaming it?'

'It's no dream, my love.' His mouth claimed hers with a passion that threatened to drain her, his tongue exploring her soft receptive moistness. Terri clung to him as though afraid to let him go—and his kiss was so thorough that by the time he had finished she was gasping for breath.

'Does that prove I'm sincere?' His smile was infinitely tender, at complete odds to the depths of desire ravaging his eyes. They had darkened considerably, causing Terri's throat to constrict each time she looked at them. She had never seen him so disturbed. It was an exciting and heady thought that she was able to do this to him. Kiel had always struck her as a man in complete control of himself. That no one would ever be able to shake him out of that self-inflicted cool.

She nodded shakily.

He held her against him, his heart banging against his rock-hard chest, her own echoing in response. She felt safe in his arms, as though she had found a haven, a shelter from the storm that had ravaged ever since she arrived in the Lakes.

She loved Kiel, deeply and permanently, and at this exact moment her happiness knew no bounds. 'I never dared hope you'd feel like this about me.' Her voice was muffled against his chest.

'I was fascinated by you right from the moment we first met,' he said softly. 'I admired your independence. It was one of the biggest disappointments of my life when I discovered that you and Barry were——'

'Friends,' she finished for him, her voice firm.

He grinned. 'That wasn't what I thought at the time! It was one hell of a shock to my system. You didn't look like that type of girl, but what else was I to think?'

'And now you know better?'

There was only the slightest hesitation before he nodded. 'But if I've made a mistake and I catch you and Barry together again, I'll kill him—*and you!*'

The venom in his voice shocked Terri and she pulled out of his embrace. 'I thought you trusted me?' There was pain in her wide violet eyes, her happiness fading as rapidly as it had grown.

'It's my stepbrother I don't trust—he can be very persuasive, believe me.'

Terri closed her eyes. Kiel's mercurial changes of mood were frightening. Just as she had thought everything was going well between them he had spoilt it.

Whe she looked at him again he was back to normal, a wry smile twisting his lips. 'I can't help it, Teresa. I shall never change my mind about Barry. But it was unfair of me to put you in the same class. Hell, let's go, this is no place for an argument—or to make love. And I know which I'd prefer at this moment!'

He turned reluctantly and started the engine, pausing for just a second to rest his hand reassuringly on her thigh before easing the powerful car back into the line of traffic.

Terri had not realised how busy the road was. Now she wondered how many people had observed their heated lovemaking. Not that she cared, she loved Kiel so deeply that she was not ashamed.

She rested her own hand on her leg where his had been, a self-satisfied smile on her lips. Her whole body was on fire, and she needed the time between now and reaching his parents' home to come down to earth.

Yet with Kiel at her side how was that possible? She did not feel she would ever be the same again. He had changed her whole life. There was a future now where there had been none before. He had not actually said that he loved her, but she didn't care. Their relationship had taken an enormous step forward—it was enough for the time being.

There was still a feeling of delirious happiness coursing through her veins when they reached the Allens' cottage. Neither had spoken during the remainder of the journey, each content in the knowledge that their feelings were mutual.

Now Kiél smiled and took her hand. Together they walked up the path. Pamela opened the door before they reached it, a welcoming smile on her lips.

'I hope you don't mind an extra guest for lunch, Mother?' he said. 'I've brought my future wife.'

CHAPTER TEN

TERRI was as shocked as Mrs Allen. She glanced quickly at Kiel, accepted the kiss he dropped on her brow, returned the pressure of his hand, but inside felt as bewildered as a fawn who has lost its mother.

The older woman recovered sufficiently to beam her pleasure. 'This is wonderful news. You're a dark horse, Kiel, and no mistake. I never dreamt you felt like this about Terri.'

'Nor did she,' he grinned. 'But I had to be sure.'

'Come along in, let's tell James.' Pamela was bubbling with joy. 'He'll be tickled pink. Like me, he once made the very natural mistake of thinking Barry and Terri were——' She tailed off, missing Kiel's thunderous glare. 'But Terri put me right about that straight away.' She sighed happily. 'James—where are you? Kiel and Terri are here. They have something to tell you. Drat that man, he's always missing when you want him!'

'Tending his roses?' suggested Terri with a smile. 'We'll go and find him.'

'And I'll put the kettle on,' said Pamela.

'Mother,' said Kiel with mock ferocity, 'I think our engagement calls for more than tea. Where's that champagne you keep hidden away for special occasions?'

James, too, was delighted, and the whole day passed in a blur of happiness.

'Do you know,' said Kiel's mother to Terri, 'I thought he was going to remain a bachelor all his life. I'd given up all thoughts of him getting married.'

Kiel flicked her an amused glance. 'I was simply waiting for the right woman to come along.' He smiled fondly at Terri. 'I knew the second I stopped to change your wheel that you were the one.'

'Me too,' whispered Terri shyly.

Pamela and James exchanged happy glances.

On their way home Terri posed the question that had been puzzling her considerably for the last few hours. 'Why didn't you tell me it was marriage you had in mind? I was so surprised when you told your mother I nearly gave the game away.'

'I didn't know myself until that moment,' he said nonchalantly. 'At least, I was sure I wanted to marry you, but I wasn't so sure you'd agree.'

'So you presented me with a *fait accompli*? Without making a fool of myself I couldn't back out?'

He slanted her a lazy smile. 'I wouldn't say that. You're a girl who knows very much her own mind. If you hadn't wanted to marry me you'd have said so whether my mother was present or not.'

How well he knew her! 'One thing worries me, though,' she said. 'The last time I was at your mother's, I overheard you telling her that you were only being nice to me because you couldn't bear to work at daggers drawn with someone. How do I know this isn't part of the same plot?'

He groaned. 'It wasn't you I was talking about, you silly sweet idiot, it was Barry. My mother thought I'd had a change of heart because I'd made him such a generous loan. Not likely! It was just to get him out of my hair. It was my stepbrother I couldn't bear to work with. He was ruining my chances with you.'

He was silent for a moment, then he said in a deeply disturbing voice, 'How about coming back to my house? There's no reason why we shouldn't spend the night together, not now? I'm sure you don't like being alone in the flat. I remember how nervous you were when you first came. How about it, Teresa? Please say yes. It means so much to me.'

Terri wanted to agree, desperately, even the very thought of it set her inside on fire. But her innate morality made her shake her head. 'I'm sorry, Kiel, I couldn't.'

'Why?' His head jerked, his frown faintly visible in the fading daylight. 'You think I'm not serious about wanting to marry you? You think I'm after an affair?' An edge of anger tempered his voice, making Terri squirm uncomfortably in her seat.

'Of course not, but—well—I want to, Kiel, I really do, but I don't think we ought to—sleep together—not until we're married. I might be old-fashioned, but——'

'You sure are,' he grated testily. 'Who the hell gives a damn in this day and age?' Then he visibly relaxed. 'But I admire your convictions. You're right, of course. I'm just thinking of myself. I want you so desperately, Teresa, it's driving me insane. I don't know how I've held back all these weeks.'

'Nor I,' she whispered, 'but it will be all the sweeter when the time comes, don't you agree?'

He did not reply and she glanced at him anxiously. 'Kiel, are you angry?' There was certainly a grim line to his jaw, and he was concentrating more fiercely than was surely necessary on the road ahead.

'Only with myself,' he said. 'I should never have suggested it. I've just realised how easily I could have lost you. It would have served me right if you'd told me to get lost.'

'Kiel, I wouldn't do that.' Terri touched his leg, feeling the muscles tense beneath her fingertips. 'I—I love you, and that's why I want to do things right.'

He grabbed her hand, squeezing it painfully tight. 'You're one in a million, Teresa. I don't deserve you.'

He let her go as he swerved to miss a pheasant and they were silent for the rest of the journey.

When they neared the turning to his home, Terri almost asked him to take it and drive up to the house, but she knew she was right in sticking to her principles, and the moment passed.

He stopped outside the surgery, kissed her good night, then sat and watched as she mounted the steps and opened the door. He did not offer to come in, and Terri was grateful, because the atmosphere between them had become so volatile there was no saying what would happen.

She appreciated him accepting her refusal, and blew him a kiss from the doorway before going inside.

As she lay in bed that night Terri had never felt happier. All her dreams were coming true. Marriage to Kiel was the one thing she would have asked for had she been told she could have a single wish granted. It was magical; it was exciting. This was the happiest day in her life.

And yet at the back of her mind she was troubled by the fact that Kiel had not actually said he loved her. But surely he would not have suggested marriage if he didn't? Then why hadn't he told her? It was a big step to take if all he was after was a physical affair. He *must* love her.

It was a long time before she went to sleep. The events of the day whirled round and round in her mind like the fragments in a kaleidoscope and when she eventually sank into oblivion she still had not reached any satisfactory conclusion.

The next morning she pushed her misgivings to one side and prepared for her meeting with Kiel. They had planned to have lunch out and then go for a long drive. He wanted to show her more of the Lakes.

Terri's heart raced as she showered and dressed, choosing a pretty pink summer dress which complemented the translucency of her skin.

Long before Kiel was due to arrive she was ready. When his knock came on the door she flung it open, a ready smile on her lips. It faded when she saw Michael West. So much for her hope that she had finally convinced him he was wasting his time.

Michael was as tall as Kiel, but without his powerful physique. His black hair was short and neat and it looked as though he was growing a moustache.

'What's the matter, aren't you pleased to see me?'

He took a step towards her and Terri backed. 'What are you doing here?'

'Now there's a welcome!' he said plaintively. 'Do you realise what time I set out this morning?'

He looked hurt and Terri felt immediately sorry. But she had no intention of giving him an enthusiastic greeting. She had not invited him here, nor did she want him. 'Why didn't you let me know you were coming?'

'I wanted to surprise you,' he grinned.

He had done that all right. He had *shocked* her. 'But I might not have been in.'

He smiled patiently. 'I'd have waited. I'd wait all day for you, Terri, you should know that. Aren't you going to ask me inside?'

She pulled a wry face. 'Of course,' and stepped back, wondering at the same time what Kiel would say when he discovered she had a visitor. It would certainly ruin their day out because she could not very well turn her back on Michael when he had come all this way especially to see her.

'You've certainly shut yourself away from it all,'

said Michael. 'I thought I was never going to find you.'

'I like it,' said Terri defensively. 'It's—a change. Did Richard give you my address?'

He nodded. 'Barry happened to phone while I was visiting your brother. Richard mentioned that he'd moved on and I thought you might be lonely. I thought I might persuade you to come back.'

He moved towards her, his expression pleading. 'I miss you like hell, Terri. I can't believe that you're truly happy here?'

'How can you miss me when you're away so much?' Terri deliberately crossed to the other side of the room, eyeing him warily, hoping that he was not going to prove too much of a nuisance.

'But there was always you to come back to.'

Terri would not have put it that way herself. She was there, yes, but not waiting for him. He was the proverbial thorn in her side, blind to the fact that his feelings were not returned.

She had lost count of the number of times he had declared his love, blithely insisting that she would learn to love him too if she'd let herself. His confidence was to be admired, but a waste of time so far as she was concerned.

'Michael,' she said plaintively, 'you know you've never meant as much to me as I do you, and I'm sorry, but there's really nothing I can do about it. You shouldn't have come. I don't want to hurt you, but——'

'You'll never change your mind?' he suggested ruefully. 'I thought that maybe absence would make the heart grow fonder. It's been so long, Terri. I missed you dreadfully while I was in Venezuela. I couldn't wait to get home. It shattered me when I discovered you'd moved—permanently.'

His eyes were doleful as they rested on her face, making Terri feel as though she were to blame. But he should have known. She had her own life to live after all. Couldn't he see that? Why did he keep pestering her?

'Even when I phoned and you told me how happy you were here I couldn't help hoping. That's why I've come to see you. Darling, Terri, you can't do this to me. I love you desperately. I want you to marry me.'

If it hadn't been so embarrassing it would have been funny. Two offers of marriage in the same number of days! Michael had never asked her to marry him before, even though she knew he always had it in mind. He had been waiting for her to return his feelings. She wondered how she could deal with the situation tactfully, without causing him any more distress.

'Michael,' she said, slowly moving back towards him, 'what can I say? I'm flattered, and I really do wish I could give you the answer you want. But things haven't changed. You know how I feel about you. I like you, I like you a lot. But I don't——'

'Love me,' he finished for her. 'You could learn, I know you could. You never give yourself a chance. Always you fight shy. Is it your own emotions you're afraid of, Terri?' He took her shoulders, sadness reflected in his eyes. 'I'll never harm you. You can come to me in your own time, you know that. I'll never force myself on you.'

She felt sad. Michael would never light her fires. His touch meant nothing. He and Barry alike were both her friends, but no more. Why was it that men could not accept a platonic friendship? Why did they have to spoil everything by demanding something physical?

Kiel was the only man she wanted to give herself to,

wholeheartedly, without reservation. It had been her destiny from the moment they met. Perhaps love always happened like that? A lightning bolt out of the blue. Kiel meant everything to her. If she didn't marry Kiel she would marry no one. It was that simple.

But there was no way she could explain this to Michael. He would never understand, not in a thousand years. 'You're making things very difficult for me.' Terri's wide violet eyes were sad as they looked into his. 'I wish I loved you, honestly I do. I hate hurting you. Why can't you accept that—oh, excuse me.'

The telephone ringing gave her the excuse she needed to put an end to the conversation.

'Teresa, my love.' Kiel's low sensual growl sent shivers down Terri's spine. 'I hate to tell you this, but I've been called out. I shall be a bit late.'

She dared not admit it was a relief, but it did give her chance to get rid of Michael. 'Are we still going out to lunch? If not, don't worry, I can——'

'I'll be there. Now I must go. I'll be as quick as I can.'

The line went dead and Terri replaced the receiver slowly. Michael was watching her. 'Who was that?'

'Dr Braden.'

He frowned. 'You're having lunch with him?'

Terri nodded.

His lips firmed. 'Is this a regular thing?'

'No,' she said quickly. At least she could give an honest answer. This was only the second occasion she had had Sunday lunch with Kiel.

'You could have told him I was here.' Michael's eyes were pained. 'I've booked into a hotel in Windermere. I was hoping to spend some time with you.'

'Oh, Michael, wasn't that rather foolish?'

'I didn't think so—at the time,' he said stiffly. 'What's wrong, Terri? Am I interrupting something? Is this Dr Braden the real reason you're so keen to stay up here?'

Terri looked down at her hands. There was no point in lying. 'As a matter of fact, yes, he is. But I enjoy my job as well,' she added defensively.

Michael shook his head sadly. 'Terri, I hope you're not going to make the same mistake as you did with Greg?'

'This is different,' she said at once. 'I love Kiel. He's the right man for me. I have no doubt about that.'

'You thought you loved Greg.'

'You sound exactly like Richard,' she said angrily. 'Why don't any of you men think I'm capable of running my own life? I came up here to get away from you all.'

A muscle jerked in his jaw and Terri wished she hadn't made that last statement. But it was too late to take it back and apologising would only make things worse.

'If you must know,' she said quietly, 'Kiel has asked me to marry him, and I've agreed. This time I shall not change my mind. He's the man I've been waiting for all my life.'

His brows lifted sceptically. 'You really have got it bad, haven't you? But you can't possibly be sure, not on so short an acquaintance. How long have you been up here, three weeks, four?'

Terri shrugged. 'Time doesn't enter into it. I just know he's the man I want to spend the rest of my life with. Because I made one mistake it doesn't mean I shall make another.'

'I can see there's nothing I can say that will make you change your mind.' There was resignation on

Michael's face now, a sadness shadowing his eyes. 'I deliberately stayed in Venezuela much longer than necessary to give you time to miss me. I thought maybe that was what was wrong with our relationship, I was always around. I wish now I'd never gone. I'd never have let you throw up your job and come here.'

'I'm sorry.' Terri's voice was no more than a whisper. 'Truly, I am. I do love you, Michael, but only as a friend. I wanted to create a new life for myself, away from everybody. I didn't know I'd fall in love. I wasn't looking for it.'

He searched her face thoroughly, but clearly could not find what he wanted. With a heartrending sigh, he turned away. 'How about a cup of coffee and then I'll go? I'll leave you to get on with your life.'

Terri nodded silently and moved to plug in the kettle. She felt really sorry for Michael, but knew there were no words which would help. He had to accept the fact that she would never be his. He ought to have done so long ago.

But she wasn't heartless, she knew exactly what he was going through. Hadn't she felt the same when she thought Kiel did not love her? She could easily have been condemned to a lifetime's unhappiness, just the same as Michael.

All these years she had known there was never anyone else for Michael except her, but she had not really cared, had not realised how badly he was suffering. Now she knew—and he had her deepest sympathy.

They drank their coffee in silence. Terri had never seen Michael look so defeated. 'Are you still going to stay on here?' she asked softly.

He shrugged. 'I don't know what I'm going to do yet. I probably will hang around for a few days. I might as well have a look what's on offer. But don't worry, I won't bother you again. It crucified me seeing you with Greg. I don't think I could stand the pain of watching it happen all over again.'

Terri winced, but knew it was best this way.

He was on the verge of leaving when he said, 'Terri, if things don't work out—I'm not saying they won't. I hope they do, for your sake. I want you to be happy. That's the most important thing in my life, your happiness. But if, for any reason, you need help, someone to turn to, you know where I am.' He kissed her then, a tender prolonged kiss, that revealed his agony and saddened Terri, so that when he finally left her eyes were moist and she felt acutely depressed.

She sat down and immediately jumped up again as she heard voices through her open window. Looking down she saw that Kiel had arrived.

Why couldn't he have been another couple of minutes later? she thought. She had not wanted the two men to meet, at least not at this stage of her relationship. Kiel was unpredictable. He might like Michael and accept him as a friend of hers, on the other hand he could quite easily misinterpret the whole affair.

And this was exactly what it looked like. His brow was thunderous, his stance aggressive. Their words drifted up to her as the conversation became more heated.

'I don't suppose she told you about Greg, either? The guy she was once engaged to.' Michael's face was flushed, his fists clenched. Terri had never seen him so angry.

Kiel's head jerked back as though the other man had delivered a blow. 'No, I didn't know. Tell me more.'

Terri groaned and raced out of the room, desperate to put a stop to things. Michael had no right telling

Kiel about her past life. It was over, done with, nothing to do with anyone now.

'Kiel!' She ran down the steps. 'We're going to be late if——' Her voice faltered and stopped. His eyes were full of pure hatred as he swivelled to confront her, his face hard and white and evil.

She went cold inside, glancing swiftly from him to Michael, who gave her a swift sympathetic smile, and then back again. 'Kiel?' Her tiny voice sounded as shrivelled as her heart.

'The best thing you can do, Miss Denning, is go back to London with lover-boy here.'

'But——'

'You fooled me completely.' He ignored her interruption. 'I see now that my first impressions were correct. It would be interesting to find out exactly how many guys you've taken in with those big violet eyes and that purer-than-driven-snow expression. But I think I've heard enough.'

He swung round to Michael. 'Take her, and welcome.' The hard edge to his voice sliced through the warm summer air like a sword. 'If you've come all this way to see her you obviously don't care what sort of a girl she is. Who knows, perhaps you're two for a pair.'

'Kiel,' protested Terri, her voice anguished, 'you must listen. You're wrong—oh, so wrong. I love you. I never loved anyone else.'

'Not even this fiancé I was told nothing about?'

'I thought I did, but——'

'And you think you love me? Is that it? Well, hard luck, because I don't love you. I want you out of here, now, this minute.'

'But, Kiel!' Tears streamed down Terri's cheeks as he leapt into his car. She stepped forward. She had to make him see sense. He couldn't go, not like this, not without talking the whole thing over. He couldn't! She wouldn't let him.

He rammed the car into gear and surged forward, as Terri frantically tried to stop him. The next moment she was knocked off balance. As she hit the ground a pain shot through her head, followed by a roar like thunder in her ears, and then nothing.

CHAPTER ELEVEN

TERRI was aware of a hand holding hers, but it was too much of an effort to open her eyes. It was a warm, strong hand, firm fingers stroking soothingly, except that it was not her hand that needed soothing, it was her head. It hurt intolerably. Even the very act of trying to think made it worse.

Kiel's name was often on her lips as she drifted in and out of consciousness. 'Kiel—hate—not love—Kiel—hate—*hate*—HATE.' The pain of knowing he hated her pierced even her comatose state.

She thought she saw him sitting beside the bed, but when she managed to force open her eyes it was Michael.

'Terri!' His voice was no more than a shaky whisper. 'Thank God!'

Then a nurse appeared. 'Welcome back. You've given us all quite a fright!'

Back from where? wondered Terri, her brow creasing. She moved her head but pain seared. She touched it and felt a bandage. What had happened? She was in hospital, but why?

And then it all came pouring back. Kiel hated her. He had told her to get out of his life.

'Kiel—where is he?' she managed to husk.

Michael frowned. 'You want to see him?'

'*No!*' Oh, God, her head hurt so much. She wanted to go back to sleep. There was escape there from this pain in her head, in her heart. Her heart was broken too, did anyone know that? Had they a cure for broken hearts? 'I want—to go home,' she whispered.

'In good time,' said the nurse firmly. 'We have to get you better first.'

'How long?' mouthed Terri.

'I can't say. You'll have to ask the doctor.'

The doctor! Kiel? She frowned again, wincing as pain stabbed through her, darting Michael an anxious glance.

'Dr Bulman,' he told her, guessing the reason for her anxiety. 'He'll be in to see you shortly. He'll tell you what you want to know.'

Terri closed her eyes and felt herself fading back into oblivion. She was glad. It was safer this way. Thoughts were painful. Too painful.

When she awoke, she lay for a long time with her eyes closed, marshalling her thoughts into order, finally accepting that Kiel no longer wanted her. He had misconstrued entirely what Michael had told him, but that did not matter. If he couldn't accept her at face value, then he was not worth bothering about.

'Terri, are you awake?' Michael's gentle voice broke into her thoughts. She looked at him and smiled faintly. 'You're still here?'

'I'll always be around when you need me,' he said.

'You're so kind.' She struggled to sit up. The pain in her head was not so intense. 'I'll try to get better quickly. I can't have you neglecting your work because of me.'

He shook his head. 'It's not important. You are. How are you feeling? You look much better. At least you've got some colour in your cheeks. You've looked like a ghost these past few days. I've been so worried.'

'Have I been here long?' frowned Terri.

'Four days. You've been in a coma. Do you remember what happened?'

Terri inclined her head a fraction, pain filling her

eyes, not physical pain but mental anguish, which she guessed would be with her for the rest of her life.

It would fade in time, she knew that, she would learn to live with her unhappiness, but at this moment it hurt as much as her head.

'I'm sorry,' he said. 'If I hadn't come chasing up here it would never have happened.'

Terri touched his hand. 'Please, Michael, don't blame yourself. Kiel never truly trusted me. He used to think that Barry and I were lovers. I don't think he ever really accepted that we were no more than friends. You turning up finally convinced him that——' she swallowed tightly, 'that I'm no good. He's probably wondering how many more there are I haven't told him about.'

Michael pulled a wry face. 'Why didn't I keep my big mouth shut? But he made me so mad. He asked who I was and when I told him I was a friend of yours he really laid into me. He's one hell of a jealous man, Terri. I didn't like what I saw and I didn't want you to tie yourself to him—that's why I told him about Greg as well. I guessed he'd see red and finish things between you, but I never imagined it would have such terrible consequences.'

'Perhaps you've done me a favour. Who knows? He'd have been a very difficult man to live with, I know that. His lightning changes of mood were sometimes frightening.'

In the days that followed Michael spent most of his time with her. Barry came, Richard and Rachel visited her, but Kiel she never saw. She discovered that he was paying for her private treatment, but she didn't feel grateful. It was the least he could do. It was his fault she was here. If his conscience was bothering him then she felt glad.

But she grew more and more despondent by his

absence, even though she did her best to hide her feelings. Michael knew her well enough to guess at her thoughts, and was careful not to bring Kiel into their conversation.

On the day she was due to leave Michael went to fetch her belongings from the flat. She sat on the edge of the bed waiting, unable to stem the feeling of sadness that stole over her.

It would not have hurt Kiel to come and see her, just once. Did he still hate her so much?

She turned when she heard footsteps, glad it had not taken Michael long. She wanted to be away from the Lakes, back home to the safety of London. There was nothing left for her here, except heartache.

Then she saw Kiel. The change in him was dramatic. He looked positively haggard; his cheeks pale and drawn, his eyes bleak with none of the vitality she normally associated with him.

He hovered in the doorway, clearly unsure of his reception, and this again was unlike the Kiel she knew. She wondered whether he was ill. There was definitely something wrong with him.

'I understand you're going back to London today?'

She nodded, turning away, unable to look any longer at the man who hated her so much he had tried to kill her.

'Teresa.' He moved into the room, his footsteps soft—and *stealthy*! Her heartbeats quickened, and she whirled to face him, unconsciously putting her hands to her throat in a self-protective gesture.

Pain filled his face. 'Teresa, I'm not going to hurt you. I know how you feel, but I had to come and see you for one last time. I don't expect you to forgive me, I just want to say I'm sorry, for—everything.'

Terri shrugged. 'You always made it pretty plain

what you thought of me. I should have known it was too good to be true when you asked me to marry you.'

'It would have worked,' he said, 'if it hadn't been for my insane jealousy. I couldn't bear to think any other man had touched you.'

She noticed he used the past tense, and although she had known their engagement was over it hurt to hear it from his own lips. 'You make it sound as though I've slept around with every man I've met!' she challenged, trying to be bitter and angry, but too conscious of Kiel's magnetism, which still came across as strong as ever. Whatever he did to her, whatever he said, it would make no difference to her love for him.

He shook his head. 'Don't be ridiculous. But I'm disappointed you didn't tell me about Michael, or that guy you were engaged to. Hearing it like I did made me see red.'

'Would it have made any difference if I'd told you?' she demanded. 'Wouldn't it have ended things even more speedily?' Her sudden flare of aggression died. 'Besides,' she added sadly, 'there was nothing to tell.

'Michael is a lifelong friend, a neighbour. He's always had a crush on me, but I've never felt anything for him. He just keeps trying. I feel sorry for him. And Greg, well, he was a mistake, I admit. He swept me off my feet. I really thought I was in love. It was just after my parents died and I needed someone. I soon came to my senses. Barry you know about. And that's the sum total of my love life, apart from the odd date which never led to anything.'

Kiel sat down suddenly on the edge of the bed, his head resting in his hands. 'Do you know, it doesn't matter to me any more what you've done. You can have had a dozen lovers for all I care. I've been pretty foolish. I should have accepted you as I found you—a genuine, warm-hearted, refreshing girl—not what I thought you were. It was you knowing Barry that did it, of course. I've met a few of his girls—and a pretty bad lot they were. I'm afraid I tarred you with the same brush.'

He lifted his head and looked at her, his eyes red-rimmed and desolate. There was no hatred, no hostility. He looked as though he had the weight of the world on his shoulders.

Terri did not know what to say. He had admitted he was wrong, but did not appear to want to try and patch things up. She grimaced. 'Like I said, Barry was more my brother's friend than mine, even though he did try it on a couple of times. I certainly never gave him any encouragement.'

'You're not the type to encourage any man, unless he means something to you. I know that now. But when you responded to my kisses I couldn't accept that it was me alone you were reacting to, I chose to believe you were like that with all men.' He swallowed painfully. 'And now I've hurt you so much that I've destroyed your love.' His head fell again, shoulders hunched.

Faint hope sparked inside Terri. 'I—I've never stopped loving you, Kiel,' she whispered.

He became motionless, as though waiting to hear what she had to say next.

'You can't help how you feel, jealousy is an emotion that's very difficult to handle. But I don't hold it against you. When you almost ran me over—you weren't in control. You were——'

'*Terri!*' He sat up so violently he made her jump.

'You didn't know what you were doing,' she said.

'I damn well did know!' he shouted. 'I would never harm a hair on your head, the one person I love more than anything in the world no matter how angry I was.

I just don't know how it happened. I never saw you. I honestly never saw you.'

Terri's head began to spin. It was all too much in her weakened state. 'Kiel, I——' she began, and then fell in a dead faint in his arms.

She was out for a few seconds only, coming round to discover herself lying in the bed, Kiel bending over her, his eyes anxious, his hands touching her cheeks.

'Hell, I'm sorry,' he said. 'You've been ill, you need gentle handling. Was I such a swine to you?'

'No,' she said, smiling. 'You were you.'

'And did I hear you right when you said you still loved me?'

'Yes,' faintly, shyly.

'You don't hate me?'

'No! Never!'

'But I heard you say it?' A frown creased the space between his brows. 'When you were coming out of your coma you distinctly said that you hated me. Why do you think I've kept away from you all this time? Hell, you don't know how hard it's been. Fortunately I was in the position of being able to get a full progress report, otherwise I think I'd have gone mad.'

'Oh, Kiel, you idiot! I remember—I was dreaming or delirious, or something. But I didn't say that *I* hated you—but that *you* hated me. You were there?'

He grimaced. 'All the time, until you said that. What a pretty mess we've made of things between us! Thank God it's sorted out.' And then, anxiously, 'It is, isn't it? You will still marry me?'

'If you'll have me.' Her wide amethyst eyes rested lovingly on his face.

'I don't deserve you. You ought to give me a good hearty kick in the pants and tell me to be on my way.'

'I might just do that,' she said, 'if I have any more of these jealous freak-outs.'

Kiel looked serious all of a sudden. 'I promise you, I'll never be jealous again. If you can still love me after all I've put you through, then the least I can do is trust you. You can have as many *platonic* boy-friends as you wish. I'll never doubt you.'

Terri snaked her arms around the back of his neck. 'I don't want anyone else, just you, for ever and ever.'

'Amen,' he said quietly.

Neither saw Michael return with her suitcase. He smiled gently but ruefully, placed it on the floor and tiptoed back out of the room. Terri had found her happiness.

Mills & Boon

Take 4
Exciting Books
Absolutely
FREE

Love, romance, intrigue... all are captured for you by Mills & Boon's top-selling authors. By becoming a regular reader of Mills & Boon's Romances you can enjoy 6 superb new titles every month plus a whole range of special benefits: your very own personal membership card, a free monthly newsletter packed with recipes, competitions, exclusive book offers and a monthly guide to the stars, plus extra bargain offers and big cash savings.

**AND an Introductory FREE GIFT for YOU.
Turn over the page for details.**

As a special introduction we will send you four exciting Mills & Boon Romances Free and without obligation when you complete and return this coupon.

At the same time we will reserve a subscription to Mills & Boon Reader Service for you. Every month, you will receive 6 of the very latest novels by leading Romantic Fiction authors, delivered direct to your door. You don't pay extra for delivery — postage and packing is always completely Free. There is no obligation or commitment — you can cancel your subscription at any time.

You have nothing to lose and a whole world of romance to gain.

Just fill in and post the coupon today to **MILLS & BOON READER SERVICE, FREEPOST, P.O. BOX 236, CROYDON, SURREY CR9 9EL.**

Please Note:- READERS IN SOUTH AFRICA write to Independent Book Services P.T.Y., Postbag X3010, Randburg 2125, S. Africa

FREE BOOKS CERTIFICATE

To: Mills & Boon Reader Service, FREEPOST, P.O. Box 236, Croydon, Surrey CR9 9EL.

Please send me, free and without obligation, four Mills & Boon Romances, and reserve a Reader Service Subscription for me. If I decide to subscribe I shall, from the beginning of the month following my free parcel of books, receive six new books each month for £6.60, post and packing free. If I decide not to subscribe, I shall write to you within 10 days. The free books are mine to keep in any case. I understand that I may cancel my subscription at any time simply by writing to you. I am over 18 years of age.

Please write in BLOCK CAPITALS.

Signature _____

Name _____

Address _____

_____ Post code _____

SEND NO MONEY — TAKE NO RISKS.

Please don't forget to include your Postcode.

Remember, postcodes speed delivery. Offer applies in UK only and is not valid to present subscribers. Mills & Boon reserve the right to exercise discretion in granting membership. If price changes are necessary you will be notified.

6R   Offer expires July 31st 1986.

EP86